Step into the world of NYC Angels

Looking out over Central Park,
the Angel Mendez Children's Hospital,
affectionately known as Angel's,
is famed throughout America for being at the
forefront of paediatric medicine, with talented
staff who always go that extra mile for their
little patients. Their lives are full of highs,
lows, drama and emotion.

In the city that never sleeps, the life-saving
docs at Angel's Hospital work hard, play hard
and love even harder. There's *always* time
for some sizzling after-hours romance…

And striding the halls of the hospital,
leaving a sea of fluttering hearts behind him,
is the dangerously charismatic new head of
neurosurgery Alejandro Rodriguez. But there's
one woman, paediatrician Layla Woods, who's
left an indelible mark on his no-go-area heart.
Expect their reunion to be explosive!

NYC Angels

*Children's doctors who work hard and love
even harder…in the city that never sleeps!*

Dear Reader

Okay, I'll admit it. I'm a sucker for a cowboy. I mean, really, there's just something about a gorgeous man in a cowboy hat that makes my heart go thump-thump-thumpity-thump. Make that man gorgeous, good-hearted and the owner of a sexy Texan drawl and I might just have to turn up the AC. Tyler Donaldson is just such a man. Ty was my first cowboy hero, but I seriously doubt he'll be my last. I had a lot of fun researching his character. Really, I did. Have I mentioned how much I love my job?

Ty and Ellie's story also presented me with another new experience as this was my first continuity series. Working closer with my fellow Medical Romance™ authors was great, and I loved watching as each of our stories developed. What an amazingly talented group!

I hope you enjoy Ty and Ellie's story as much as I enjoyed researching (grin!) and writing their story. Drop me an e-mail at Janice@janicelynn.net to share your thoughts about their romance, cowboys or just to say hello.

Happy reading!

Janice

NYC ANGELS: HEIRESS'S BABY SCANDAL

BY
JANICE LYNN

MILLS & BOON™

To my editor, Lucy Gilmour. Thanks for all you do!

First published in Great Britain 2013
by Mills & Boon, an imprint of Harlequin (UK) Limited.
Large Print edition 2013
Harlequin (UK) Limited, Eton House,
18-24 Paradise Road, Richmond, Surrey TW9 1SR

© Harlequin Books S.A. 2013

Special thanks and acknowledgement are given
to Janice Lynn for her contribution to the
NYC Angels series

ISBN: 978 0 263 23128 1

Harlequin (UK) policy is to use papers that are
natural, renewable and recyclable products and made
from wood grown in sustainable forests. The logging
and manufacturing process conform to the legal
environmental regulations of the country of origin.

Printed and bound in Great Britain
by CPI Antony Rowe, Chippenham, Wiltshire

Janice Lynn has a Masters in Nursing from Vanderbilt University, and works as a nurse practitioner in a family practice. She lives in the southern United States with her husband, their four children, their Jack Russell—appropriately named Trouble—and a lot of unnamed dust bunnies that have moved in since she started her writing career.

To find out more about Janice and her writing visit www.janicelynn.com

Recent titles by the same author:

CHALLENGING THE NURSE'S RULES
FLIRTING WITH THE SOCIETY DOCTOR
DOCTOR'S DAMSEL IN DISTRESS
THE NURSE WHO SAVED CHRISTMAS
OFFICER, GENTLEMAN…SURGEON!
DR DI ANGELO'S BABY BOMBSHELL
PLAYBOY SURGEON, TOP-NOTCH DAD

These books are also available in eBook format from www.millsandboon.co.uk

Janice won
The National Readers' Choice Award
for her first book
THE DOCTOR'S PREGNANCY BOMBSHELL

NYC Angels

Children's doctors who work hard and love even harder...
in the city that never sleeps!

For the next four months, step into the world of NYC Angels

In March New York's most notoriously sinful bachelor Jack Carter
finds a woman he wants to spend more than just one night with in:
NYC ANGELS: REDEEMING THE PLAYBOY
by Carol Marinelli

And reluctant socialite Eleanor Aston makes the gossip headlines
when the paparazzi discover her baby bombshell:
NYC ANGELS: HEIRESS'S BABY SCANDAL
by Janice Lynn

In April cheery physiotherapist Molly Shriver melts the icy
barricades around hotshot surgeon Dan Morris's damaged heart in:
NYC ANGELS: UNMASKING DR SERIOUS
by Laura Iding

And Lucy Edwards is finally tempted to let neurosurgeon
Ryan O'Doherty in. But their fragile relationship will need
to survive her most difficult revelation yet...
NYC ANGELS: THE WALLFLOWER'S SECRET
by Susan Carlisle

Then, in May, newly single (and strictly off-limits!)
Chloe Jenkins makes it very difficult for drop-dead-gorgeous
Brad Davis to resist temptation...!
NYC ANGELS: FLIRTING WITH DANGER
by Tina Beckett

And after meeting single dad Lewis Jackson, tough-cookie Head
Nurse Scarlet Miller wonders if she's finally met her match...
NYC ANGELS: TEMPTING NURSE SCARLET
by Wendy S. Marcus

Finally join us in June, when bubbly new nurse Polly Seymour
is the ray of sunshine brooding doc Johnny Griffin needs in:
NYC ANGELS: MAKING THE SURGEON SMILE
by Lynne Marshall

And Alex Rodriguez and Layla Woods come back into each other's
orbit, trying to fool the buzzing hospital grapevine that the spark
between them has died. But can they convince each other?
NYC ANGELS: AN EXPLOSIVE REUNION
by Alison Roberts

Be captivated by NYC Angels in this new eight-book continuity
from Mills & Boon® Medical Romance™.

CHAPTER ONE

UH-UH. THERE WAS absolutely no way Dr. Eleanor Aston was wearing that itsy-bitsy, teeny-tiny scrap of sparkly spandex her sister had sent for her to wear tonight!

"Take it back," she ordered Norma, the darling, elderly woman who'd headed up the Aston household for over twenty years and a woman who was more like family than—well, than Eleanor's biological family.

Looking out of place and uncomfortable in the hospital doctors' lounge where Eleanor had pulled her to talk in private, Norma shook her head. "Sorry, but I can't do that. Brooke gave me specific instructions. You are to wear that dress and those shoes to the ribbon-cutting ceremony."

Right, because she could squeeze her more than generous curves into the dress. Eleanor shuddered just at the mental image.

"I'm giving you specific instructions, too. Take it back, because even if I could squeeze into that…" She eyed the glitzy red dress and matching stilettos her sister had picked out. "Well, it's not exactly my style, is it?"

Staring at Eleanor with her almost-black eyes, Norma shrugged her coat-clad shoulders. "Perhaps your sister thinks your style needs an update."

Norma's tone implied that Brooke wasn't the only one who thought that.

Ha. No doubt about it. Media darling Brooke Aston definitely thought her sister's style as ugly duckling in the midst of a family of swans should change. Mostly because Brooke thought Eleanor's usual wardrobe of hospital scrubs to be the bottom of fashion's totem pole.

Eleanor loved her hospital scrubs.

For so many reasons. Never had she felt more proud than when she'd donned a pair after she'd completed her training as a pediatrician specializing in neonatology. Plus, shapeless hospital scrubs hid a lot of body flaws.

"A lot" being the key words. She'd never be a size two like Brooke and she'd quit beating herself up over that years ago.

She eyed the scrap of fancy material again, crinkled her nose and shook her head. "I'm sorry my sister wasted your time, but you can keep the dress because I'm not going to wear it, or those torture devices my sister calls shoes." She glanced at her watch. "Sorry to run, but I've got to get back to the NICU. My patients need me."

Norma winced, but didn't look surprised by Eleanor's answer. "Brooke won't be happy."

Was her baby sister ever happy with anything that didn't involve all the attention being on her? Too bad she'd had an allergic reaction to some new beauty cream that had left her unable to bask in the limelight of Senator Cole Aston's latest publicity project.

At least this time Eleanor agreed with how her father was spending his money. Actually, she was quite pleased, which was the only reason she'd agreed to take Brooke's place at the ribboncutting ceremony this evening. He'd donated an exorbitant amount to build a new neonatal wing for premature babies at the Angel Mendez Children's Hospital where she worked.

She loved being a part of something as wonderful as Angel's, New York's first and finest free children's hospital. Working with her preemies left her with a feeling inside that no other aspect of her life had ever achieved. She felt needed, whole, as if she made a difference. In her patients' families' eyes, she did matter, was the most important person in their tiny baby's world.

Her patients didn't care that she wasn't glamorous or wearing the latest Paris styles. They didn't care if her hair was plain black and always clipped tightly to her scalp in a bun. They didn't care that she never bothered with makeup or taking time to put in her contact lenses so her thick-framed glasses didn't hide her dark brown eyes.

Neither did they care that she'd never be beautiful and svelte like her petite sister, not with her bone structure and too-generous curves that no amount of starving herself seemed to cure. So she just maintained a healthy diet and lifestyle and ignored that the media liked to point out the differences between her and her Hollywood-thin, perfectly coiffed sister.

Pain knotted Eleanor's gut at the recall of some of the comments that the gossip rags had made about those differences over the years.

Her sister might love the limelight, but Eleanor detested it, did everything she could to avoid putting herself in the media's glare. Yet tonight she would be representing her family at a very important event for Angel's. The press would be there in droves.

What had she been thinking?

The sheer impact of what she'd agreed to do hit her, made her hand shake, reminded her that she was being forced to attend a social event. Still, think of all the families the new wing would benefit.

She took a deep breath, praying a full-blown panic attack didn't hit. "Brooke isn't going to be happy anyway, Norma. She's not the one cutting the ribbon this evening."

Having been a constant fixture in their lives and knowing them as well as their own mother did, probably better, a semblance of a smile played on Norma's twitching lips at Eleanor's accurate assessment of her sister.

"Agreed, but you're going to have to return that dress yourself." At Eleanor's frown, she continued, "If I'm going to have one or the other of you upset with me, it's going to be you over your drama-queen sister."

Eleanor took another deep breath and exhaled slowly. Hadn't it been that way her whole life? Brooke always managed to get her way one way or another, whether it was with their parents, the hired help, the media, or the many enamored people who flocked to be close to such "perfection" as the lovely and superfun Brooke Aston.

Eleanor had spent a great portion of her life in the shadows. Fortunately, she liked it there.

She glanced at her watch again. She'd been away from the neonatal unit too long already. "Fine. I'll deal with this later."

* * *

Eleanor's heart squeezed as Rochelle Black-wood's tiny fingers wrapped around her pinky finger. So precious.

Even with the tubes and wires attached to the twenty-six-weeks-gestation little girl, nothing was more beautiful or precious to Eleanor than new life.

Not so many years ago, Rochelle wouldn't have had any chance of surviving outside her mother's womb short of a miracle. Thanks to advances in modern medicine, the little girl's odds had greatly increased, although certainly she was high risk. Still, each day she survived raised those odds.

Eleanor intended to give her tiny patient everything in her favor that she could.

"What do you think, Eleanor?" Scarlet Miller, the head neonatal unit nurse, asked from beside the tiny heated incubator. "Is she going to pull through?"

Rochelle had been born with part of her intestines outside her abdomen, with underdeveloped lungs and eyelids that were paper-thin and not yet open. She couldn't eat or breathe on her own. But the little girl had a strong will to live. Eleanor felt the strength of her spirit every time she was near the baby.

"I hope so. She's a fighter, that's for sure."

Rochelle's mother had been sideswiped by a drunk driver and had suffered multiple crush injuries. Rochelle had been in trouble and the decision had been made to deliver by emergency cesarean section. Sadly, her mother hadn't survived the night.

Eleanor felt a special bond with the baby, perhaps because the five-day-old baby's father was grieving the loss of his wife and had yet to visit the little girl who'd already undergone multiple surgeries and treatments during her short life. The medical staff of the NICU was the only human contact the baby had.

"Agreed," a strong masculine Texan voice drawled from behind her. "I hope you don't mind, but I've been keeping tabs on this little darlin'."

As it always did when Dr. Tyler Donaldson was around, Eleanor's face caught fire. Not literally, of course, but it may as well have for how hot her skin burned anytime the man was near.

Just as it also always did, her tongue refused to do anything other than stick to the roof of her mouth, leaving her unable to answer him and feeling like an awkward teenager with a first crush.

Urgh. How could one sister be such a consummate flirt and known for the many hunks wrapped around her manicured finger and the other sister be a shy, inept mute just because a good-looking man spoke to her? Not even spoke to her about anything personal but about a patient. Yes, she really was pathetic.

Probably taking her silence as disapproval—or who knew what he thought of her since he usually ignored her—Tyler stepped closer to the incubator. "I was on duty the night she made her entrance into the world. She's such a sweet little darlin', ain't she?"

His Southern accent got to her, just as it did

most of Angel's female staff. In a big way. His voice was so inviting, like a fire on a cold winter's night. She just wanted to bask in the warmth of everything about the man. Which was crazy. He was a total player who charmed women right out of their pants. Yet all his exes still adored him. Go figure.

She risked a look at him and immediately wished she hadn't. Just as if she really did stand next to a fire, her face burst into a new wave of flames. If there was a pill to cure blushing she'd be first in line at the pharmacy, because she hated the nervous reaction almost as much as she hated her panic attacks.

"You met her father?" Tyler asked, his warm brown gaze focused on the baby.

Still unable to prise her tongue off the roof of her mouth, Eleanor shook her head.

"Guess he still ain't been by." Tyler sighed, making the sound long and as drawn out as his speech, as if every sound that came from his mouth had to stretch the span of his home state of Texas. "Can't help but feel bad for the guy.

Losing his wife that way and afraid that he'll lose this li'l sweetheart, too."

Her tongue still not cooperating, Eleanor nodded.

"I'm glad she got assigned to you, Eleanor. She got lucky and got the best." Without looking up, he brushed his finger gently across where the baby still clung to Eleanor's finger.

Sparks shot up her arm and her breath caught in her throat.

She'd been so engrossed in the man beside her, in his unexpected compliment, she'd completely forgotten she was still touching the baby until his skin made contact with hers.

Wow.

Just wow.

Thinking she had finally prised her tongue loose, she turned to try to say something witty, but just as she opened her mouth, he flashed that half-crooked grin of his. At someone walking up beside them.

Someone else female.

Because he was Dr. Tyler Donaldson and that's what he did best.

With every single female in the NICU except for dumpy, boring, *mute,* too-curvy Eleanor Aston.

Where was the black dress she'd brought with her that morning?

Panic raced through Eleanor as she stared at the contents of her staff locker.

It had been ransacked.

In the place of her gym bag, the black dress that she'd neatly hung that morning and the pair of black flats she'd planned to quickly change into was a note in familiar handwriting.

A note that made smoke billow from her ears.

You're gonna look so hot, sis. You can thank me later. B.

Thank her? Ha. She was going to strangle her sister. How had Brooke gotten into the doctors' lounge? Gotten into her locked locker? Not that her sister had been there herself. No way would

Brooke risk being seen or photographed with her face red, swollen and peeling.

Yet her sister had wiped her out.

Even her purse was gone.

There were three items in the locker other than the note. The red dress and stilettos that her sister had so thoughtfully sent over and a square white box that covered almost the entire bottom of the locker.

Dare she even open the lid to see what lay inside?

She glanced at her watch, knew she was running out of time and snatched the lid off to stare at the items inside.

Underwear. Eleanor wrinkled her nose. Leave it to her sister to know that if you were going to wear an itty-bitty dress you had to have itty-bitty underwear to go with it.

Plus, a red clutch purse that matched her dress and shoes and a too-big, too-flamboyant hair clip meant more for adornment than to actually be useful.

And makeup. Lots of makeup.

Acid gurgling in her stomach, Eleanor shook her head. This was her place of employment, the hospital where she worked.

Okay, she'd jump in the shower and pray that when she was clean, her belongings would be back.

They weren't.

"What's wrong?" Scarlet asked, doing a mad make-over dash of her own to get changed for the ribbon-cutting.

"My sister has gone too far this time." Eleanor tightened the towel she had wrapped around her body. "How am I ever going to be taken seriously again if I wear that?"

Scarlet's gaze ran over the dress then over Eleanor from head to toe. "I'm pretty sure if you wear that there's going to be a lot of people taking you seriously. Maybe one person in particular."

Eleanor's chest tightened. "What do you mean?"

"Don't give me that. I've seen how you look at him."

"Who?" Had her voice just squeaked?

Scarlet laughed. "Dr. Donaldson."

"He barely knows I exist."

Scarlet motioned to the dress. "You wear that and there's not going to be a man alive who isn't aware you exist."

Eleanor crinkled her nose. Brooke she could see putting her into a dress she shouldn't be in, but she trusted Scarlet. "You really think so?"

Scarlet gave her a *duh* look. "Hurry up and get changed and I'll help you do your makeup and hair. You have great eyes and hair. We'll play them up to draw attention to them."

Great eyes and hair? Right. Had Brooke bribed her friend to say that? Next thing she would be telling her she had a great body.

"Of course, with a chest like yours it's going to be difficult to keep attention anywhere but on your cleavage."

That she knew. Which was why she never wore anything revealing or clingy. Her breasts were too big, but they matched her curvy hips and thighs.

But Scarlet was right. She was running out of time and it wasn't as if she had anything else to wear. Plus, she felt ridiculous talking while wearing only a towel.

She let her gaze go back to the items in her locker. If she was going to look a fool, she might as well go for broke. "Why not?" She smiled at her friend. "We'd better hurry. Thanks to my father for being out of town and Brooke not being able to make it, yours truly is sort of the guest of honor."

"You're going to totally knock the socks off Dr. Donaldson," Scarlet mused as Eleanor stepped into the dress. "It's a perfect fit."

Eleanor blinked, then put her glasses on and stared at herself in the mirror. "Yeah, but where's the rest of the dress?"

She tugged on the material, trying to cover some of her cleavage, but only managed to hike the skirt higher up her thighs.

Dear Lord, if she bent over someone might get a glimpse of those tiny scraps of underwear

Brooke had left her no choice but to wear or go commando.

Mortification set in. "I can't go out in public like this."

Scarlet inspected her then nodded. "You're right. Hand 'em over."

"Huh?"

"Your glasses. Give them to me."

One hand protectively holding on to her frames, Eleanor shook her head. "I can't see without them."

Scarlet tsked. "You should get contact lenses. You have gorgeous eyes."

"I have contacts." She wore them for sports and exercise, but rarely when she was at the hospital as she was more comfortable behind the shield of her glasses. "But since my sister took my purse, I couldn't put them in if I wanted to."

"Not a problem." Before Eleanor could stop her, Scarlet had plucked her glasses off her face and refused to give them back. "Now, let's get you to the ribbon-cutting because you're already five minutes late."

Eleanor glanced at her arm, realized she wasn't wearing her watch and frowned. Late? The senator was not going to be happy with his elder daughter.

During the whole walk to the new wing, Eleanor told herself that all the stares she was getting was because she was wearing a fancy red dress in a children's hospital.

She knew better.

Thank goodness she'd decided to carry her heels because if she'd had to walk in those things over to the new wing, she'd have fallen flat on her face and probably split the seams of her dress in the process.

"Quit fidgeting," Scarlet ordered from beside her. "You look great."

She looked a fool—not that she could see how foolish she looked, not without her glasses.

Only this time was much worse than past embarrassments because she was at the hospital where she worked, surrounded by the people she worked with, people who, until today, had respected her as Dr. Eleanor Aston.

* * *

Dr. Tyler Donaldson grinned at the cute little nurse who worked in the obstetrics department and considered the possibilities.

Just as he knew she was sizing him up.

No doubt she'd heard about his reputation.

Everyone at the hospital knew he was a love-'em-and-leave-'em kind of man.

He liked it that way. Truthfully, he was pretty sure most of the women liked it that way, too, although they'd never admit it.

He was a good time waiting to happen, but not a keeper.

However, the blonde was looking at him as if she wouldn't mind keeping him occupied for the night.

"I can't believe Dr. Aston isn't here yet," she chattered, although Ty was more interested in what her eyes were saying. Those eyes were saying *you and me, bub, hot and sweaty between the sheets*.

Although he hated admitting it, lately he'd been getting bored with women.

"I never would have thought she'd be late."

Dr. Aston? No, he wouldn't have pictured her the type to be late either. She seemed much too uptight to be anything other than punctual. Unless something had come up with one of her tiny patients and then Ty could see the dedicated pediatrician blowing this celebration altogether. He'd be hard-pressed to name a more dedicated doctor.

"It's so difficult to believe she and Brooke Aston are really sisters."

He'd have to live in another country not to know who Brooke Aston was. The media loved her. The image of a blonde bombshell came to mind. Yeah, accepting that the two women came from the same DNA pool was difficult to believe.

"Brooke was supposed to have been here to cut the ribbon, but she caught a virus or something while volunteering at some charity event for sick children," the blonde prattled on. "I hope it's nothing serious."

From the things Ty had seen about the infamous senator's daughter, he had a hard time envisioning her getting close enough to sick kids to have actually caught something from them.

"Maybe one of them was adopted," he suggested to make polite conversation. With the publicity for the new wing, he'd heard about the family connection prior to this evening. As Eleanor didn't make a bleep on his possibility radar, he hadn't paid much attention to the hospital gossip.

But something about her irked him. He couldn't quite put his finger on what it was about her, just that he'd decided to steer clear.

"Oh, my word!"

At her gasp, Ty's attention jerked back from thoughts of a woman who crept into his mind more often than a woman who didn't make a bleep on his radar should to the OB nurse. Her gaze was fixed beyond him to the hallway leading into the new wing. He turned to see what she was looking at and found his own breath catching in his throat.

It took him only a moment to realize who he

was looking at. Even then he had to do a double take before he could convince himself that he wasn't wrong. But once he realized that it was really *her,* his chest tightened, making him gulp for much-needed oxygen.

"I don't believe it," the nurse next to him muttered. Neither did Ty.

He didn't believe he'd totally missed that Dr. Eleanor Aston had been hiding a killer curvy body beneath those baggy scrubs she wore. Wow.

Bleep. Bleep. Bleep.

Hell, what was his possibility radar doing? He was not interested in Eleanor. Not in baggy scrubs or in a body-hugging red dress that ought to be labeled lethal. Not with her gorgeous brown eyes wide and uncertain rather than hidden behind her glasses as she faced the crowd. Not with her glossy black hair flowing loosely down her back rather than tightly pinned to her scalp.

Only he was and maybe he had been all along.

Bleep.

CHAPTER TWO

"I'M SORRY I'M LATE," Eleanor apologized to the hospital CEO, to the hospital medical director, to the NICU director and several other hospital bigwigs whose titles she couldn't quite recall. "I—I worked, and then I had to shower and change." She glanced down at her barely there dress and way-too-exposed body as if that explained everything. "And then my sister had…"

She stopped, realizing she was rambling, realizing that they all stared at her as if she'd grown a second head and spoke in foreign tongue. Or maybe they were all staring at her too-ample bosom overflowing out of Brooke's idea of a sick joke.

Eleanor couldn't be sure because she couldn't see any of their faces clearly. Which was probably a good thing because she was pretty sure disapproval marred their expressions. They'd never take her or her suggestions for the hospital seriously again.

"Dr. Aston, how do you feel about your father donating the money for the new wing?" A man poked a microphone in her face.

Bile pooled in her stomach. The press. She'd known she'd have to deal with them, both at the ribbon-cutting and at the reception afterward. She wanted to shrivel up and become invisible in the hope they'd go away and not notice her.

Fat chance of that when she was essentially the guest of honor.

Not her, really. Just Senator Cole Aston's daughter.

Which technically she was, but if someone had told her she'd been accidentally swapped at birth, she'd have no trouble believing them as she was so different from her socialite mother, power-hungry father and media-darling sister.

She much preferred being Dr. Eleanor Aston, who was someone she was proud to be most of the time.

She didn't feel proud at the moment.

She felt awkward and uncomfortable and like she might throw up.

She looked at the reporter, wanted to be like Brooke and deliver a smooth, witty line about how proud she was of her father for making such a wonderful contribution to the hospital and community.

But she wasn't Brooke and under the best of circumstances she wasn't witty.

Half-naked and surrounded by people who'd once dubbed her "Jelly Ellie" didn't come close to being the best of circumstances.

Why had the bane of her childhood reared its ugly head now? For years she'd kept that much-used media label out of her head. She wouldn't let it back in, wouldn't let the slurs back into her mind, wouldn't let them degrade the woman she'd become. So she wasn't a skinny Minny and never would be. She was average, of healthy weight and her curves were fairly toned thanks to the hours she spent in the gym each week. The press could get over their craze for too thin.

Thankfully, the hospital CEO grabbed her by

her elbow and whisked her toward the ribbon that partitioned the new wing from the rest of the hospital. A big bright red ribbon that perfectly matched her dress. Had Brooke planned that? Probably. Her sister had an eye for detail.

"We're already a little behind schedule." The CEO didn't actually say that it was her fault but she felt the weight of his implication all the same. He was getting his slam in on Dr. Eleanor Aston being late, but wasn't going to say anything specific to Eleanor Aston, daughter of Senator Cole Aston. "So we'll get the show on the road."

Fine. The sooner they got this started, the sooner they'd finish, the sooner she could go home and try to figure out how she was ever going to face her coworkers again.

Wondering if everyone could see how her legs were shaking, Eleanor stood next to the CEO while he droned on and on about the hospital and what a blessing it was in the community.

Then he did something horrible. He turned

to Eleanor to give a welcome-and-thank-you speech.

Immediately, the full-blown panic attack she'd been fighting most of the day took over. Her heart picked up pace, doubling in tempo. A hot sweat broke out on her skin, making her palms immediately feel sticky wet. Her tongue attached itself to the roof of her mouth and refused to budge.

She took a deep breath, reminded herself that the rapid pounding of her heart was just anxiety and not that her heart was really going to explode from fear of being in the spotlight.

Although the blonde at his side felt it necessary to continue to chat softly to him, Ty's attention was focused solely on the woman standing next to her bosses. His bosses.

In direct opposition to the low-cut-cleavage and long-leg-revealing dress, her ethereal face looked fragile, pale, out of place.

Ty didn't have to see the pulse jumping at the

base of her throat or the tremor of her knees to know she was nervous.

Nervous? More like petrified.

She appeared as delicate as a butterfly's wing and just as beautiful with those big brown eyes of hers and that full mouth.

A mouth made for kissing.

She'd always kept to herself so much that he'd taken it as a sign that she wasn't interested.

Was it possible he'd mistaken shyness for disinterest?

She stirred something within him, but he'd just labeled it as curiosity, considering she was the only female he knew who didn't fall into flirt mode whenever he was near.

He was definitely curious. Beyond curious.

More like intrigued by the plethora of contradictions that defined his colleague.

The CEO waited for Eleanor to speak.

The rest of the crowd waited for her to give her speech.

A too-long pause settled over the crowd.

"H-hello. It—it is…" A few stuttered words

began escaping her quivering lips. "An honor… an honor to be here. Today. This evening, I mean."

"She sure isn't her sister," a man next to Ty with a camera in his hands grumbled under his breath.

Surprisingly, Ty's fingers curled, the man's comment rubbing him up the wrong way. Why he felt so protective of a woman he wasn't certain he even liked, he had no clue. But he found himself wanting to speak up, to defend her. How could you defend someone you didn't really know?

Still, he shot the man a silencing look. "Not everyone is a polished speaker, but Eleanor is a fantastic doctor and woman."

The man's bushy brows drew together then he shrugged. "Whatever, pal." Then he went back to snapping photos.

Not looking anyone in particular in the eye, Eleanor began speaking again, and Ty found himself letting out a breath he hadn't realized he'd been holding.

"Th-thanks to everyone for coming to this wonderful occasion where we're celebrating the opening of a new neonatal wing at the Angel Mendez Children's Hospital." She paused, swallowed hard, then smiled what he knew was a forced smile before she continued. "M-many of you know pediatrician Federico Mendez started this hospital during the depression after the death of his much-loved son, Angel, who suffered from polio. My father, Senator Cole Aston, wishes to continue the tradition started by Federico Mendez."

Her expression tightened and she cleared her throat, pausing too long yet again.

Come on, Eleanor, he mentally willed her on. *Just thank everyone for coming again and be done.*

"It is with that same generous and caring spirit that my father donated the funds for this new neonatal wing in the hope that—that..." Between stutters, she thanked everyone for coming to the ribbon-cutting. Then, not seeming to know what else to say, she turned imploring eyes on the CEO.

Imploring eyes because she was begging to be rescued.

How was it possible that a woman who'd had to grow up in the public eye could be so socially backward? Surely Cole Aston would have enrolled her in some prep courses to prepare her for public speaking?

And the stuttering? Was that lifelong or something she just did when she was nervous?

Tyler wished he knew. Wished he knew lots of things about the enigma showcased in a flashy red dress.

Rather than rescuing her, the CEO looked as if he had no clue at how on edge she was. Instead, he made another big hoo-ha, then handed Eleanor a large pair of showy scissors.

Immediately, she almost dropped them but managed to recover in the nick of time. One of the men beside her rolled his eyes. Ty saw red and not just the red of Eleanor's hot dress and cheeks.

His gaze shot back to hers, saw the fear, saw the shaking of her hands, the sheen of perspiration that glistened on her skin. Something moved inside him.

Literally, something in his chest shifted.

Dear heavens, she was going to pass out.

Ty might be known as a womanizing son of a gun, but he was a chivalrous son of a gun. His momma, God bless her big Southern heart, would have beaten his hind end otherwise, and rightly so.

He might have left his horse in Texas but, hell, no one else was stepping in to save the good doctor.

Despite the fact that he was feeling a little off-kilter himself at just what a knockout body she'd been hiding under her scrubs, at whatever that odd sensation in his chest had been when he'd looked at her just a moment ago, at admitting to himself that he'd been interested in her all along, playing the role of white knight to Eleanor's damsel in distress came as natural as counting one, two, three.

* * *

Eleanor couldn't breathe.

Couldn't move.

Wasn't even sure how she was hanging on to the scissors that she'd somehow managed to position over the ribbon.

All she had to do was close her hands and the ribbon would slice.

So why weren't her fingers cooperating? Why weren't they closing around the handle?

She needed cooperation, needed to get out of there before she toppled over on her face or sagged to a humiliating puddle at the feet of her bosses. Not to mention that her dress would burst wide open if she made any sudden movements. Wouldn't the press have a field day with that?

Jelly Ellie's belly exposed yet again.

She winced, fought back the horrible thought of the photo of her happy, pudgy, eight-year-old self hanging out of her bathing suit while hugging her cute and cuddly little sister forever captured by the paparazzi. She reminded herself she wasn't that little girl anymore who'd been crushed by their cruel jokes and taglines that she carried too much weight. She was an accomplished woman, a doctor. She could do this.

Make the cut. Just squeeze your fingers together and cut the ribbon.

Nothing happened. Except that her palms grew more and more clammy. Any second the scissors were going to slip out of her sweaty hands and fall to the floor.

Headlines around the city would read *Senator Cole Aston's daughter doesn't make the cut.* Folks would nod their heads in agreement, make comments that they'd known she wasn't good enough to get the job done, that had the lovely Brooke Aston been there all would have been well.

"Dr. Aston?" the CEO prompted from beside her, his low tone warning for her to get on with the program.

She wanted to. Really, she did. But panic had seized her and, except for the trembling within her, she stood frozen in place.

The room began to spin, to darken. She was going down. She'd be mortified. Her father would blame her. Brooke would blame her. The hospital would blame her.

She prayed that when she went down she would bump her head and lose her memory, that she'd lose all recall of the day's events. Amnesia would be a blessing.

But rather than fall to the floor, a strong pair of hands closed over hers, applying pressure and closing her fingers over the scissors handles. The ribbon split in two and each end drifted toward the floor in a dainty float that Eleanor watched as if in a surreal dream.

The sound of the applause and cheers—and was that a sigh of relief?—came from some far-away surreal place, too.

When she turned her head and looked up into the twinkling brown eyes of her savior, she was definitely somewhere other than reality.

Because Tyler Donaldson winked at her and drawled a breathy, "Hi, there, darlin'."

As if it was the most natural thing in the world

for his hands to be over hers, he motioned his head slightly toward the crowd. "Better paste a smile on that pretty face of yours 'cause there are a lot of folks capturing the moment for posterity."

Who was this man and what had he done with the real Dr. Donaldson, who never spoke except in regard to patients?

She gawked at him a second longer, then turned and forced a smile to her face the same way she'd done a hundred times before. She thought of happy times. Thought of medical school and how hard she'd worked, at how proud she'd been to accomplish something her daddy's money and power couldn't buy, something she'd had to do on her own. Something that didn't require glamour, glitz or a hot little body.

Although her smile stayed on her face, her mind didn't go to her happy place. Oh, no. Her happy place was all tangled up in Tyler's hand still covering hers, holding hers, of the electricity and warmth burning into her at his touch.

He gave a squeeze as if he wanted to reassure

her that she was going to be okay, that he was there and wouldn't let her fall on her face.

Oddly enough, she believed he wouldn't.

Which was crazy. He flustered her, barely knew she existed, so how could he possibly be rescuing her from total mortification?

Her knees weakened, and she swayed.

Tyler's hand immediately went to her waist, steadying her, resting low on her back. "Just smile, babe. You're doing just fine. It's almost over."

Easy for him to say. She had to face the reception afterward, mingle with the bigwigs while representing her father, her family.

But Tyler didn't leave her side.

He stayed and smiled right there with her. He kept his hand at her back and his strength gave her the fortitude to keep her smile in place even though she really just wanted to curl up into a ball and cry.

When the photographers finally had their shots and moved on to their next victim, Eleanor let out a long breath and looked at her rescuer.

"Th-thank you."

One side of his mouth lifted crookedly in a half grin. "No problem, sugar. You looked like you needed a helping hand."

Speaking of hand, his still rested against the curve of her back, burning through the thin red material and branding her skin.

"I don't like crowds." Were those the first words she'd ever actually formed around him without stuttering, grunting or mumbling? Finally, coherency.

"I noticed."

She smiled despite the nervousness still chipping away at her resolve. "Now, if only this party were over."

"Over?" He glanced around at the smiling, laughing people and shook his head. "Why would we want the party over when the night is so young?"

"I don't like crowds, remember?" She crinkled her nose and frowned up at him. Goodness, the man was tall. Probably about six-four. Maybe everything that came from Texas was big.

He grinned down at her, then tweaked her nose with the tip of his finger. "I tell ya what, darlin', you just relax. Have some fun. I'll handle the crowd."

She glanced around at the people making their way into the room that had been decked out for the celebration. "But surely you have someone with you? You always have someone with you."

"You're right. I do." He winked then leaned close to her ear. "Tonight that someone is you, Eleanor. My friends call me Ty, by the way, and you and I are definitely going to be friendly."

CHAPTER THREE

ELEANOR LAUGHED OUT LOUD for what seemed like the hundredth time that evening. Honestly, she couldn't recall the last time she'd laughed so much.

Had she ever?

"You are very pretty when you laugh, Eleanor."

Now, there was a comment worth laughing at.

"Because you keep saying funny things," she told Tyler, not quite meeting his eyes. He'd complimented her repeatedly during the evening. Good thing she knew his reputation, that he was an incurable flirt.

With a grin that was way too intoxicating, he touched her face. "I want you to laugh at what I say, but only when I'm saying something worth laughing at. I was serious. You are a very beautiful woman, Eleanor."

Despite the fact that she was sure he didn't mean her to laugh, she couldn't suppress the nervous little giggle that spilled from her lips. "Yeah, well, th-thank you."

Because, really, what else could she say?

"Tell me about that," he urged in a slow drawl.

She bit her lower lip, hoping he wasn't asking what she thought he was asking.

"Your stutter."

Face flaming, she shook her head. "Nothing funny about my stuttering so let's not talk about it."

"Have you always stuttered?" he asked, as if she hadn't just spoken.

"Perhaps you didn't hear what I just said. I don't want to talk about me."

"But I do. You fascinate me."

Had he been drinking? The hospital wasn't serving anything alcoholic, but perhaps someone had spiked the punch.

"When I was younger, I—I stuttered all the time. These days it usually only h-happens when I'm in a stressful sit-situation."

He studied her a moment. "Am I a stressful situation?"

"Men are always stressful," she answered flippantly, because she didn't want to label anything at all about the way Tyler made her feel. Not the way he'd made her feel before tonight and especially not the way he was making her feel at that very moment.

He leaned his long frame against the hospital wall they stood near, crossed his arms and regarded her. "Ya know, I just realized that during the entire time I've been at Angel's I've never heard a thing about you and a man, Eleanor. Is there someone special in your life?"

Had the room suddenly grown hot? Her skin had certainly grown clammy.

"Not at the moment."

"Lucky me."

Not sure what to say, Eleanor glanced around the lobby that had been converted into a reception area for tonight's gathering. The crowd had started to thin and most of the press had left.

"I should probably quit monopolizing your

company," she said, realizing that he hadn't left her side the entire evening.

"Please don't, darlin'."

She glanced up at him.

"I want you monopolizing my…company."

Her breath caught. He was flirting with her. Really flirting. If she'd had any doubts earlier, now she didn't.

The only problem was that Tyler Donaldson flirting with her was way out of her league. As in she wouldn't know how to flirt back if her life depended on it.

So she just smiled and took a sip of her punch.

He had the audacity to laugh, causing her gaze to return to him. When their eyes met, she found herself laughing back.

She wasn't sure exactly what they were laughing at, but a giddy happiness flowed through her, along with a shared connection with Dr. Tyler Donaldson that was both unexpected, a bit magical and so exciting she could barely breathe.

"Who's the hunk?"

Totally lost as to what Brooke meant, Eleanor

glared at her sister across the Aston penthouse's breakfast table. Brooke's face was masked by a thick layer of medicated cream.

Eleanor had gotten up that morning determined to accomplish one thing. To kill her sister.

Not literally.

Maybe.

But seriously, Brooke had gone too far this time. Even though the night had turned out nothing short of wonderful thanks to Ty, that didn't mean Brooke wasn't going to get an earful.

"Don't try changing the subject," she warned, tapping her finger against the glass tabletop covering the rich mahogany. "You broke into a hospital doctors' lounge and stole my clothes."

"I," her sister put great emphasis on the pronoun, "didn't do anything. And don't change the subject." Brooke's head bobbed with attitude, which should have come across as ridiculous, with her platinum hair tied up and flying every which way, thick white cream covering her still-swollen face and her body wrapped in a fuzzy

pink terry-cloth robe, but which somehow didn't look ridiculous at all.

Even while suffering from an allergic reaction, her sister managed to pull off cool.

Brooke slid that morning's paper across the breakfast table. "Who is he and where can I get one? He's yummy. Introduce me."

"What are you talking about?" But even as Eleanor finished asking she saw exactly what her sister referred to.

More like who her sister referred to.

Oh, no.

Oh, yes.

A photo of Eleanor and Ty was splashed across the top of the society section of one of New York's top newspapers.

Not just any photo but one that appeared to have been edited because she knew they hadn't really been looking at each other in that manner.

Okay, so she might have been looking at Ty that way because, let's face it, he was hot and *friendly*.

"Although," Brooke mused, frowning, "he's

looking at you as if he's about to sweep you off your feet and find the closest place to get you alone. Who is he?"

In the picture, he was looking at her as if he thought her the sweetest thing since chocolate syrup and he'd like to cover her in that syrup and lick her clean.

Wow. No wonder Brooke wanted to know who he was. But, no, her sister couldn't have him. Not Ty. Which was a crazy thought because if her sister wanted Ty, she'd have him. Brooke always got what she wanted. Especially when it came to men.

"It's a trick of the camera." Perhaps it really was. Although, recalling how wonderful Ty had made her feel, perhaps it wasn't. The man knew how to make a woman feel as if she were the only woman in the world. No wonder all the female staff at Angel's adored him.

"Huh?" Brooke's collagen-enhanced lips pouted. "He isn't really that scrumptious?"

"He is, but…" She trailed off, her stomach sinking. She'd meant that he hadn't really been looking at her as if he found her irresistible. Maybe he really wasn't, but he had helped her get through what had started as a horrible evening but, because of him, had ended almost feeling enchanted.

She glanced at the photo again. She was looking into Ty's face as if she found him enchanting. Although you couldn't see his hand, she knew that his palm had rested low on her back, that his thumb had traced lazy patterns over the smooth material of the red dress. That his hand had been somewhere on her body at most points during the evening. Her lower back, her arm, her hand, her face. He'd touched her almost incessantly.

Almost possessively.

He'd felt sorry for her and his Southern good manners had demanded he rescue her. That had to be it, right?

"I couldn't be more pleased."

Both girls spun as their father entered the room.

Entered? Ha. More like invaded the room. Because when Senator Cole Aston entered a room even imaginary dust took cover. A trail of servants followed, all scurrying to serve the great man his breakfast and to meet any need he might have before he could even voice his desire.

"Morning, Daddy," Brooke cooed, blowing an air kiss in his direction as she popped a bite of melon into her mouth.

Glamour girl Brooke had always been their father's favorite. Eleanor couldn't blame him. Although the "it" party girl, Brooke never went so far as to cause their father to do more than shake his head with an indulgent smile. Her, on the other hand, he just didn't understand. Why would she want to work so hard getting her medical degree when her financial security wasn't an issue? Why work such long hours at a free hospital that she collapsed exhausted into sleep night after night when she could live a life of leisure, travel at whim as her mother and sister did?

She knew she was a disappointment and had been for most of her life. She'd been the pudgy, geeky, plain-Jane misfit who'd had to stand next to her handsome, intimidating father, her elegant, classically beautiful mother and her glamorous, much-loved and ever-popular, beauty-queen sister.

Yeah, she was pretty sure she'd been swapped at birth.

There was some dull, plain, geeky family out there scratching their heads at how they'd ended up with a beauty-queen daughter who thrived on the limelight.

"I didn't realize you were back," Eleanor ventured. He'd been in Washington, D.C., in meetings all week, which was why he hadn't been able to attend the ribbon-cutting himself.

"Daddy, aren't you going to say good morning?" Brooke pouted, tucking her leg beneath her in her chair and turning more fully toward him.

For once, the senator ignored Brooke and smiled—or as close as he got when a camera wasn't present—at Eleanor. "I flew in late last night. You'll bring him to my campaign fundraiser next week, of course."

Him? Then she noticed what he carried. A

copy of the same newspaper Brooke had shoved at her. The one with the picture of her and Ty. Her father was happy about that? Really? Then again, he was probably just amazed that some man had paid attention to his elder daughter.

"He's just a friend. Not even that, really. More of an acquaintance." At the arch of his salt-and-pepper brow, Eleanor rushed on. "We work together at the hospital. He's nobody, really."

"He's somebody all right, and I want him with you at the fund-raiser."

Eleanor's gaze met her sister's. A still-pouting Brooke shrugged, obviously not having a clue what their father was talking about either.

"His family owns about half the state of Texas. If I ever throw my hat in to run for president, he'll be our ace in the hole."

She didn't know which shocked her more. That her father already had her paired off with Ty, that Ty was wealthy or that her father thought he might someday run for president.

That he'd plan her life choices around what

best garnered votes didn't shock her in the slightest. She'd dealt with that her entire life.

"How do you know anything about Dr. Donaldson?" she asked slowly, knowing she wasn't going to like his answer.

Her father's gaze narrowed slightly at her calling Ty by his proper name. "I figured the son of a gun was just after your inheritance so I called my attorney first thing this morning and had a background check run."

Because her father hadn't believed any man would want her for herself, only for her cut of the Aston fortune. Great. Had he ever had any of Brooke's many beaus checked out?

Probably not, since her sister never seemed interested in the same man for more than a week or two. Then again, perhaps the senator did have each one thoroughly investigated and perhaps that's why none of them lasted more than a week—because they weren't worthy of his precious baby girl.

"He checked out," her father announced, sounding somewhere between smug and surprised.

"You've already gotten a report on his whole life history? Wow. That was fast work." Head spinning, she took a deep breath. "Well, you wasted your time and money, because Dr. Donaldson is a colleague from work." Sure, they'd had a great time the night before, but it wasn't as if she expected him to actually call and ask her out. They were friends. Sort of. "Nothing more."

Not liking being ignored, Brooke tapped the newspaper picture again. "This doesn't look like just work."

Her father smiled in that way that didn't convey happiness, just arrogance that he was right and that he would get his way because he was Senator Cole Aston. "I should have known you'd be contrary."

Shocked at his comment, Eleanor stared at her father. Because she was known for her contrariness? Hardly, unless he counted her going to university, getting a medical degree and actually working for a living. If he counted that then, yes, she was quite the contrary child.

"No matter." He waved his hand dismissively

then took a sip of his black coffee. "I've already taken matters into my own hands."

That didn't surprise her in the slightest. However, the implications of his comment terrified her.

"What do you mean, you've taken matters into your own hands?"

"I sent the car for Dr. Donaldson. He should be arriving…" he glanced at the slim gold watch on his wrist "…any moment."

Brooke squealed, her eyes widening. She jumped to her feet. "Daddy! You can't invite people here when my face is all messed up."

The senator ignored his younger daughter, his gaze instead boring into Eleanor. "Perhaps you'd like to go freshen up before he arrives?"

Heat rose to the tips of Eleanor's ears. Her father had sent the car for Ty? How had her father even known she'd be here? Had he cared? If her father said that he would be arriving any moment, that meant Ty had gone along with her father's request. Then again, Cole might not have requested anything. He'd probably demanded that Ty come.

Great.

She'd thought she was going to die of total mortification last night, but perhaps that honor had been saved for this morning.

Ty had ridden in a limo a few times during his life, but none of the luxurious caliber of Senator Cole Aston's. Although he definitely preferred Ole Bess, his affectionate nickname for the Ford pickup he'd driven since first getting his license, he couldn't deny that he'd been impressed.

But, then, he was pretty sure that had been Senator Aston's intention.

That and to perhaps intimidate him.

Not that Ty was easily intimidated. Only his own father seemed capable of achieving that.

Obviously, Eleanor's old man had seen the picture of his daughter with him and wanted to know his intentions.

He had no intentions.

Not toward Eleanor. Not really.

Yeah, she'd piqued his interest last night and once she'd gotten over her shyness she'd been funny and intelligent. He'd enjoyed the evening more than he would have believed possible.

He'd found her incredibly intriguing and, yes, he'd admit it, he found her sexy as hell.

But that didn't mean he had any intention of seeing Eleanor outside the hospital. Something told him she wouldn't be a love-'em-and-leave-'em-smiling kind of experience.

He didn't do any other. Which meant he should stay away from the good doctor. Which was why he hadn't made any move on her at the end of the evening, despite the fact that he'd wanted to kiss her repeatedly. Hell, he'd wanted to do a lot more than kiss her.

But he'd settled for a goodbye hug and he'd gone home alone.

The senator had nothing to worry about.

The elevator ride to the penthouse of one of Manhattan's most prestigious apartment complexes overlooking Central Park was an experience in and of itself. Ty had to smile at the seat along one wall and wondered if he was wicked for thinking of all the fun ways that seat could be used by him and…

He stopped, realizing that rather than some random hot babe popping into his head, the woman making use of that seat with him was Eleanor.

Which shocked him. Hadn't he just reminded himself that she wasn't his type?

Senator Cole Aston's daughter.

How had Eleanor ended up shy, sweet, compassionate and hardworking when she'd grown up in the lap of such luxury?

Then again, thinking about what he knew of Cole Aston, perhaps Eleanor's childhood had been more hellish than his own.

Which wasn't exactly fair, because his childhood hadn't been bad. Not really. It hadn't been until he'd gotten older, known his life was going in a different direction than his family envisioned that the problems had started with his father. The rest of his family was…things he wasn't going to think about. Not right now when he was about to get his butt chewed for latching on to Eleanor the night before.

The Aston penthouse suite was something straight out of a magazine on luxury living. The fancy living quarters probably had been featured in a magazine. Several of them. Ty almost felt as if he should take his shoes off before stepping onto the shiny hardwood floors.

Following a well-dressed woman who'd introduced herself as the head housekeeper, he entered a large room containing a long mahogany table, with Senator Aston sitting at the head and Eleanor to his right. Fresh flowers adorned the elaborately set table.

The bright red splash of color that infused Eleanor's cheeks and the quick way she averted her gaze told him she hadn't been behind his summons.

Perhaps she didn't even want him here.

Was that disappointment shooting through him?

No way. He hadn't really thought Eleanor had sent for him. He hadn't even expected her to be here as she'd told him the night before that she lived in an apartment of her own. Ty had known it was her father planning to whip out the shotgun and tell him to keep his good-ole-boy hands off his precious daughter.

No worries. He'd already decided to do that.

"Glad you could make it, Dr. Donaldson." The senator stuck out his hand and Ty shook it firmly. "Have a seat. Next to Eleanor, of course."

Senator Aston had a future in acting should he ever opt out of politics because no way was that welcoming tone real. Had he really just invited Ty to sit next to Eleanor?

Wondering what he'd gotten himself into, he sat.

"Can we get you some breakfast, son?"

Son? What the…?

"No, thank you, sir. I've already eaten."

"Coffee, tea, juice?"

What was with the host with the most?

Eleanor was now shooting daggers at her father.

"No, thanks." He searched her face, but she

wouldn't even look his way. When she finally stopped glaring at her father, she just stared at her breakfast, which it didn't look like she'd much more than touched. So he met Senator Aston's eyes and decided to cut to the chase. "You asked to see me?"

The man smiled and a shiver ran up Ty's back.

"I wanted to meet the man who spent the night with my daughter."

Ty didn't wince or glance away from the man's penetrating gaze. He wouldn't show weakness around this man who was obviously used to everyone bowing to his command. "Eleanor is a grown woman and surely makes her own choices as to who she spends her time with."

Which wasn't what he should have said. He should have pointed out that they hadn't spent the night together. Only a very public evening. Something about the man got Ty's hackles up.

"Until I saw this morning's paper I hadn't realized she was spending time with anyone," the senator countered smoothly, taking a sip from his coffee cup. "She tells me you work together."

Her shoulders having dropped at her father's words, Eleanor's face now glowed rosier than any bloom in the flower arrangement. Once again, Ty found himself feeling protective.

"Yes, she's a brilliant pediatrician. One of the best Angel's has."

Senator Aston waved off Eleanor's accomplishments and focused on the real reason he'd summoned Ty. "What are your intentions regarding my daughter?"

That's more like what he'd come expecting to hear.

"Daddy! Please." Eleanor scooted her plate back, stared at her father. "I told you that Ty and I are only work colleagues."

Ouch. Why did Eleanor's words sting?

"Ty?" Her father's brow arched, then his dark gaze settled directly on Ty in question.

Here was his opportunity to set the record straight and get the hell out of Dodge.

"It's too early to say what my intentions are regarding your daughter." Which wasn't what

he'd meant to say, but those words had somehow come out anyway.

"What?" This had come from a very shocked,
very red-faced Eleanor. "But you...you didn't..."
Her voice trailed off, not verbalizing that Ty
hadn't kissed her when they'd said goodbye.

Ty's gaze remained locked with her father's.

"I'm very protective of my daughters."

Ty bit back a grin. "I imagine so."

Eleanor's father leaned back in his chair, eyeing Ty as if he were sizing up an opponent. He
took a sip of his coffee and calmly announced,
"I want you to accompany Eleanor to my fund-
raiser ball next week."

That surprised him, but Ty only shrugged. He
wouldn't be bullied by this man. "I'm busy."

"Get unbusy," the senator ordered, as if whatever Ty's plans were they couldn't possibly be
more important than his.

"Eleanor may have other plans."

"She doesn't." Had there been humor in the
man's tone? "This is important to my career and
the perfect opportunity for me to get to know

what type of man my daughter is spending her time with."

Ty wasn't sure how he felt about going to the fund-raiser. He liked Eleanor, but hadn't he already decided that he needed to stay away from her? That she would expect more from him than he'd ever give? But there was something about the way her father was discussing her as if she weren't in the room that got Ty's hackles up, made him want to puff out his chest and stand in challenge.

What was it about the woman that gave him all these protective, testosterone-filled urges?

"I prefer to arrange my own dates."

The senator sat his coffee cup down on the table and eyed Ty intently. "Fine. Arrange one. Now is as good a time as any. I'm sure Eleanor is available the night of my fund-raiser."

"Daddy." Eleanor's voice sounded so humiliated Ty wanted to whisk her out of the room. Hell, he knew exactly how she felt. Hadn't his own father loved to put him in his place every opportunity he got?

His father. His family. Which only served to remind him of his own family issues and the fact that his mother wasn't letting up on him coming home to attend Swallow Creek's annual rodeo, which his father was hosting. Just the thought of going home, seeing the shame in his father's eyes as he expounded on what a disappointment Ty had turned out to be, turned his stomach. It would be the first time he'd be face-to-face with dear ole Dad since their big row about Ty moving to New York.

He'd be damned if he was going to face it solo when presented with such a golden opportunity.

"Fine," he agreed to the senator's suggestion, liking the idea that had struck him. "I'll go to the fund-raiser." Just as the pompous man started to smile, Ty added, "On one condition. I want Eleanor to go to Texas with me six weeks from now to attend a rodeo my family is hosting."

With her by his side, his family would be on their best behavior, would be distracted by him bringing a woman with him, and maybe, just maybe, his father wouldn't launch into how he'd screwed up his whole life and let the entire family down by following his own dreams rather than to follow in his father's footsteps.

"Done." Smiling again, the senator stuck his hand out for Ty to shake.

"What?" Eleanor's chair flew back from the table, almost toppling she stood so quickly. "Th-this is crazy. You're talking like I'm not even here." She glanced back and forth between them. "You're both crazy. I'm not going to Texas."

Wondering what the hell he was doing, Ty shook Eleanor's father's hand before any of them could come to their senses.

CHAPTER FOUR

ELEANOR AUSCULTATED ROCHELLE'S tiny chest, distinguishing each sound and praying the baby's lungs remained clear of fluid or pneumonia despite her many risk factors.

"Hey, you."

Eleanor jumped, startling the baby. Talking softly to Rochelle and stroking her finger over the baby's tiny hand, she mentally gathered her wits. What she needed was someone to talk softly to her and calm her nerves before she acknowledged who'd surprised her.

"Don't do that," she ordered, spinning to face the man she wasn't quite sure what to think of. Not that she hadn't thought of him. She'd thought of little else since yesterday morning when she hadn't been able to take any more of her father bargaining a date for her.

That she understood.

What she couldn't understand was why Ty had agreed, why he'd even suggested her going to Texas with him.

That made absolutely no sense at all to her. No matter how many times she'd tried to work out his reasons, she kept coming up blank.

Looking as gorgeous as ever, Ty grinned that sexy Southern grin that, along with his Texan drawl, had all the NICU nurses swooning over him. Eleanor's body did a little swooning of its own, too.

"Sorry, darlin'." His eyes twinkled. "Didn't mean to startle you or the babe. How's our girl doing?"

At his "our girl" Eleanor's throat clogged shut. Why, she didn't know because it was the silliest of phrases and she knew he meant their patient and… Oh, what was she prattling on in her mind for? Just answer the man and be done with it.

"She's holding her own." A complete sentence and no stutter—yeah! If nothing else, spending time with him at the ribbon-cutting and reception seemed to have cured her of that habit around him.

He nodded his understanding. "A babe's fighting spirit makes all the difference."

"Speaking of fighting spirit, why did you agree to my father's crazy suggestion that you go to his fund-raiser ball?" She tried to keep her voice light, as if his answer was no big deal. "They aren't that much fun."

He shrugged. "Maybe good ole country boy me just wanted to see what it's like to hang with the big city-slicker politicians."

Eleanor rolled her eyes. "You can cut the good-ole-country-boy act. The big city-slicker politician ran a background check and obviously liked what he found. He could probably tell me what type of baby formula you were raised on."

"I wasn't."

She stared at him in confusion. "You weren't what?"

"Raised on formula." He puffed his chest out. "My momma breast-fed me and my brother."

"I didn't need to know that." Actually, she had

a hard time envisioning Ty as a baby, as anything other than the gorgeous man he was.

"Sure you do," he countered. "Can't have you showing up in Texas as my date and not knowing a thing about me."

As his date?

"That's another thing." Her brows pulled tightly together. "Why on earth would you want me to go to Texas with you?"

He didn't seem concerned, just pulled his stethoscope out of his scrub pocket then met her gaze. "Why not? We had a nice time together at the ribbon-cutting reception and you'd be doing me a favor."

"Just as you're doing me a favor by going to my father's campaign ball?"

Ty's gaze cut to hers. "He really wasn't going to take no for an answer. I just worked a Texas travel buddy into the bargain."

"A travel buddy? If you think I'm going to—"

He held up his hand. "Stop right there. I'm not thinking any such thing, but am quite shocked at how quickly your mind went to the gutter, Eleanor." He tsked, his eyes full of naughtiness.

As much as she wanted to, she couldn't hold back her smile. "Try selling your innocence to one of your many fan clubs, Dr. Donaldson. I'm sure they'd be impressed."

His brow arched. "Not much impresses you?"

Tired of fidgeting nervously with her stethoscope, she put the tubing around her neck and shoved her hands into her lab-coat pockets. "Lots of things impress me, but not your innocence. I've seen snakes with more saintly backgrounds."

"As in the background check your father did? He couldn't have turned up anything too bad or he wouldn't have been rolling out the red carpet." His grin took on a mischievous little-boy gleam. "Sure, I tipped a few cows in my younger days, but—"

"Tipped a few cows?" She hadn't read her father's report. He'd offered, but she'd refused on principle. Perhaps she shouldn't have been so haughty.

"You should see what we did to the sheep." Ty's brows waggled.

His outlandish comment had Eleanor smothering a laugh and a few of the nurses looking their way.

"Quit distracting me from the real issue," she warned. "Why do you want me to go with you to Texas?"

This time he was the one fidgeting with his stethoscope. "I like you."

Her cheeks grew hotter than asphalt on a midsummer day. "You like me? What's that supposed to mean?"

He liked her? Not meeting Eleanor's eyes, Ty stalled by checking out Rochelle, listening to her tiny heart, lungs and surgically repaired belly, which still had various tubes and drains in place.

Very unlike him to hesitate to give an answer.

Usually he was smooth with the lines with the ladies. Usually.

Maybe it was because he wasn't exactly sure what he wanted with Eleanor that he was thrown.

That was exactly what was throwing him.

He'd decided not to pursue a relationship with her but had ended up with a date to her father's campaign ball and with her going home for the weekend with him. Not exactly consistent with staying away from her and avoiding the attraction he felt toward her.

He glanced up, studied her slightly flustered expression, uptight hairstyle, thick-framed glasses and tried to go back to seeing her as just Dr. Aston and not the intriguing woman he'd spent an evening with.

But he couldn't.

He couldn't look at her and not see beneath the surface to the woman she hid below. Couldn't not want to peel away the layers to let that woman out, to free her, and to sit back and watch the explosion.

More than watch, he wanted to experience that explosion in every shape, form and fashion.

"What are you thinking?" She licked her lips nervously.

That he wanted to lick those soft pink lips, to

taste her mouth, to take his time and kiss her all night long.

He cleared his throat. "That our girl is going to make it."

After frowning at him a moment, Eleanor took his bait and cut her gaze to the baby. "I hope so. She's such a sweetheart."

"They all are."

Surprise flickered in her gaze. "You really like babies, don't you?"

The question seemed a no-brainer to him, but he understood what she meant. A big macho Texan like him choosing to take care of babies. Could a man choose a more emasculating profession? Not according to his father. In Harold Donaldson's eyes a man might as well chop off his big boys as to "play with babies all day."

Ty didn't quite see things the way his dad did and hadn't from the point he'd realized he wanted to be a doctor. During his early academic career he'd discovered he specifically wanted to be a neonatologist. Despite his father's hee-hawing and ho-humming about the "shame of having a son who played with babies," not once had Ty felt less of a man because of his profession.

He liked what he did at Angel's, liked making a difference in his tiny patients' lives and their families' lives. He'd been blessed with a God-given talent and he was where he was supposed to be in life.

Only he had no choice but to go home for the rodeo. His mother had threatened to have the entire crew converge on him in New York if he didn't. Of course, seeing his father in downtown Manhattan might be worth it.

Then again, those skyscrapers might bow in the presence of his giant of a father.

"Ty?"

He blinked, realizing he'd totally blanked out on Eleanor. "Sorry. I got lost in my thoughts."

"I noticed." She smiled tentatively and the gesture tugged at something in his chest.

She was pretty. Why had it taken him seeing her all decked out for him to notice those eyes, that generous mouth, that porcelain skin? That phenomenal body?

"Would it help to talk about it?" she gently offered.

"Hell, no." His mother had talked about the problems between him and his father till Ty was blue in the face. Nothing was going to make his family understand his need to be a doctor.

He sure didn't want to talk about his reaction to her since the ribbon-cutting. How could he explain to her what he didn't understand himself?

"I didn't mean to pry." Obviously embarrassed, Eleanor's eyes dropped. Her chest rose and fell with a deep breath.

Ty knew his gaze shouldn't drop to watch the shifting of the material across her body, but it did. A crying shame when a grown man was jealous of a cotton scrub top, but he was.

Guilt hit him on several counts.

"Offering to listen isn't prying," he countered, smiling at her and hoping she took his peace offering. "Besides, if you're the little darlin' doing the listening, I'd be happy to give talking a whirl."

Her gaze lifted and she stared at him in confusion. A slow smile curved her lips. "You would?"

"Oh, yeah." Which surprised him, but for some reason he enjoyed talking to Eleanor, enjoyed seeing the uninhibited emotions play across her lovely face. "Go to dinner with me tonight?"

Hands digging deeper into her pockets, she eyed him suspiciously. "Is my father paying you to be nice to me? To take me out?"

Ty laughed, put his hand on her lower back and led her away from Rochelle's incubator. "Is that how your sister has a new beau every week?"

Eleanor's face lost some of its sparkle. "If you have to ask that, you obviously left my father's place without having met my sister."

Brooke hadn't made an appearance during the few minutes Ty had remained after Eleanor had disappeared.

"If she's anything like you, she's a knockout."

Eleanor's eyes rolled behind her thick-framed glasses. "Right."

"Definitely."

When had they fallen into step together?

Where were they even headed? To the new wing, he realized. More and more of the neonatal unit was being transferred to the area.

"Seriously, if it means going to dinner with you, I'd spill my guts on all the reasons why I want you to come to Texas with me."

She considered him a moment, then nodded. "Okay, Ty, you have a deal. You get to feed me and I get to listen."

"I get the better end of that deal."

Her brow lifted and she grinned with an almost flirty gleam in her dark eyes. "You haven't seen me eat."

Watching Eleanor eat should be X-rated.

Ty was positive he'd never seen a woman take so much delight in food. Most of the women he knew barely picked at the few scraps of lettuce put on their plate, much less actually enjoyed each bite with such unabashed pleasure.

He was also positive that he'd never been turned on at watching a woman eat, but he was turned on.

Majorly turned on.

Each and every time Eleanor's mouth closed around her fork, her eyes closed and joy lit up her face. Had she moaned with her delight in the food he wouldn't have been surprised.

She opened her eyes, caught him watching and pink splashed her cheeks. "Sorry."

"For?"

"Making a glutton of myself. I like to eat. I did warn you."

"Enjoying your dinner isn't making a glutton of yourself."

She pushed her plate back, eyeing the remaining food with regret. "Yeah, but if I want to fit into my dress for my dad's campaign fundraiser, I'd best stop."

Immediately his mind was brought back to the tight red dress that had wrapped around her body so delectably at the ribbon-cutting.

"You fill a dress out just fine."

"Yeah, that's the problem." She sighed a bit self-derisively. "I fill it out."

"Why is that a problem? Admittedly, I've only

seen you in one dress, but you looked great."
More than great. She'd been hot. "Ever since
then I've been considering requesting a change
to hospital policy just so I can see you in a dress
on a regular basis."

Snorting softly, she toyed with the napkin in
her lap. "You can't help yourself, can you?"

"Hmm?" he asked innocently, knowing he
hadn't been innocent since his sixteenth birth-
day when he and seventeen-year-old cheerleader
Casey Thompson had made out after a football
game.

She folded the napkin and placed it neatly in
her lap. "Whenever there's a woman around you
just have to spew out compliments."

"Is it wrong to tell a woman she looks beautiful with her glasses off so that I can see those
amazing eyes?"

Those amazing eyes lowered. "I wear my contacts for sports. I just didn't change back to my
glasses afterward, that's all. Thank you for the
compliment, but you don't have to say things
like that. I don't expect you to."

Ty considered all she'd said, trying to decide which subject he wanted to tackle. The fact that she wasn't used to compliments was the one that bugged him most, but for now he opted to go with one that would hopefully have her relaxing again. He wanted her relaxed, wanted her to enjoy their dinner as much as he was.

"What sport do you play?"

Her relief was palpable and he was glad he'd not pushed. He'd liked the easy camaraderie between them, the easy flow of conversation as they discussed everything from the new hospital wing to the New York Knicks, who, to his surprise, Eleanor loved.

"Tennis and racquetball mostly. I was on the swim team and ran track during my high-school years. I still do both, but only for the exercise."

He picked up her fork, loaded it with food and held it out to her. "Then I'd say you're allowed to finish your dinner."

Eyeing the fork of North Atlantic salmon with longing, she shook her head. "I can't."

"You can," he said temptingly, moving the fork toward her mouth.

"Really, I shouldn't." But her eyes said she wanted to.

"You should, darlin'." He brought the food to her lips and they parted. He barely bit back his groan when her eyes closed and she savored the melt-in-the-mouth entrée.

He convinced her to have dessert under the pretense of them sharing it. He enjoyed immensely having the excuse to feed her bite after bite, watching her reaction as the cheesecake hit her tongue.

Watching Eleanor Aston eat could quickly become an obsession.

"You promised me an explanation about why you wanted me to come to Texas with you," she reminded him, dabbing her mouth with her napkin.

"That I did." Somehow in the course of their dinner and the enjoyable company he'd forgotten all about the trip to Texas. That alone was testament to how wrapped up in watching Eleanor, in talking with her, he'd been. "My family is hosting the local rodeo this year. I need a date."

Her gaze narrowed suspiciously. "You're never short on dates, Ty. Why would you choose me?"

"Why wouldn't I?"

"Because we're not dating."

"One could argue that technically we're on a date at this very moment."

She seemed to consider that a moment, then met his gaze again. "I'm not your usual fare."

"Exactly."

She frowned. "What's that supposed to mean?"

He laughed at her expression, quite enjoying how her every thought was broadcast so plainly in her eyes. "Quit looking so perturbed, Ellie. I meant it as a compliment."

If anything, her frown deepened. "Don't call me that."

"What? Ellie? It fits." He spooned another bite of the cheesecake, but she wouldn't even look at it, just shook her head, practically wincing.

"I don't want any more and, no, that name doesn't fit."

He started to tempt her, knew he could, but realized there was more going on than she was telling him, something profound.

"I'll make a deal with you," he offered, watching every emotion flicker across her lovely face.

"What's that?"

Had her voice broken? Her eyes were sparkling and not from looking at him but as if she was fighting back tears.

Ty reached across the table, took her hand in his and laced their fingers. "I'll only call you Ellie when you steal my breath with your beauty."

Not looking at him, she snorted. "That's a deal I'll gladly make, because I don't want to be called that." She took a deep breath, pulled her hand free of his and slipped on what he supposed was her game face. "Now, tell me more about this trip to Texas."

Ty wanted to dig, wanted to know what made Eleanor tick, to know what had upset her, but now wasn't the time for digging for details. At least, not into Eleanor's life. His was another story altogether as he'd promised her the goods.

Eyeing Eleanor's quiet expression, he couldn't resist saying, "For the record, I wouldn't count on not hearing me call you Ellie again. You're a very beautiful woman. On the inside and the outside."

She ignored his implication and his compliment. "So the trip's for an entire weekend?"

"We'll fly up on Thursday morning and can safely sneak out on Sunday afternoon under the need to get back to our patients. Should be a breeze, right?"

Four days with Ty Donaldson. Could she survive it? Because the man was a natural-born charmer and she really wasn't equipped to deal with the likes of him. It would be so easy to believe in his quick lines.

To believe in the way he looked at her.

Because he looked at her as if he found her attractive. If she'd thought she'd imagined it the night of the ribbon-cutting, she'd been wrong.

He was looking at her the same way right this minute. As if he found her interesting, desirable, beautiful—inside and out.

When he'd fed her, she'd almost died. No man had ever fed her, ever taken pleasure in doing such a simple act, but Ty had. When she'd opened her eyes after that first bite, she'd seen the pleasure in his eyes. He'd enjoyed feeding her every bit as much as she'd enjoyed him doing so.

Don't read anything into it. You've seen how he's gone through women at the hospital. You're just this week's flavor.

"Where I come from," Ty continued, "the local rodeo is a very big deal. My brother and I grew up wanting to be rodeo stars, but we're too tall."

"Is that like one of those carnival rides where you have to be this tall to ride, only in reverse?" she teased, trying to picture Ty as a young boy.

He grinned. "You're funny. Actually, most cowboys on the rodeo circuit are under five and a half feet tall."

Her eyes widened. "That's pretty short for a man."

"But just right if you're going to ride a bronco."

If he said so. In her mind, she preferred thinking of cowboys as tall, dark, ruggedly handsome. Like Ty, actually. Which set off a whole slew of cowboy fantasies. Not good.

She could see Ty in worn jeans that fit just so, in a Stetson that sat upon his head just so, with no shirt on, of course, because in her mind he was all six-pack-and-muscle bound. And feeding her some light and flaky calorie-free delicacy that only paled in comparison to him.

She picked up her napkin, started to fan her face with it, realized what she was doing and dropped the cloth back into her lap.

"My father said you grew up on a ranch so I imagine you do ride, even if you are too tall to be a rodeo star," she said, taking a sip of her water in the hope of moistening her dry mouth and cooling her libido, which was in overdrive.

"I was riding a horse before I could walk." His grin widened, making her wonder if he could somehow read her thoughts and knew exactly the effect he was having on her body.

"Well," he continued, his eyes twinkling, "not alone, but I've seen the pictures of me sitting on a horse in one person or another's lap. Donaldsons pretty much go from birth to horse."

"What about cows?"

"Nah, we don't ride cows until we hit at least elementary-school age." His lips twisted with amusement. "My nephew's competing in the sheep-riding competition."

"Sheep-riding? How old is he?" For the life of her, Eleanor couldn't picture a wild bucking sheep trying to throw someone off its back. But what did she know about ranch life or rodeos?

"Don't look so horrified. William is four. Feel sorry for the sheep. That kid is hell on wheels."

The love in Ty's words was strong, making Eleanor wonder yet again why he'd stayed away from Texas so long. "Takes after his uncle Ty?"

"Nah, that would make him the black sheep of the family."

His answer startled Eleanor.

"I can't imagine any family not being proud of

your accomplishments." Then again, didn't her own parents look at her as if she was demented for working for a living?

"I should prepare you. My father and I had a disagreement, shall we say, about my career choice and where I chose to work."

"Because he wanted you to practice in Texas?"

Ty's face lost its playful edge. "Something like that. Quite frankly, darlin', the man scares the daylight out of me."

He said it jokingly, but there was no humor in his voice.

"Because you're easily scared?" Her fingers toyed with the napkin in her lap, twisting one end back and forth.

"There's a reason I work with babies." Although his tone was teasing, something told her there was more to what Ty said than his actual words.

"I'm glad you work with babies, Ty. You're an excellent doctor and your patients are very blessed to have you overseeing their first few months in this world."

His smile was genuine and her compliment softened his eyes. "Ditto, Ellie."

She frowned at his use of the nickname, but his grin held and he shrugged as if to say he couldn't help himself.

"A deal's a deal," he reminded her.

Right. Because he'd looked across the table at her and she'd stolen his breath by her beauty and had felt the need to let her know.

"Tell me about your brother," she rushed forward, not wanting to let her mind go down the "Ellie" path. They'd been there once too often that evening already.

"Harry is great. The spitting image of my father and the golden boy of Swallow Creek. All his life, he's excelled at everything he's done, especially bowing to my father's whims. On paper, he runs the ranch, but I've no doubt my father still pulls the strings."

His words held no sarcasm, no malice. She could tell that he genuinely loved his brother, yet so easily his words could be taken as sibling rivalry. Or worse.

"He's older?"

Ty nodded. "By three years."

She considered her next words carefully. "Must've been tough growing up in the shadow of such a successful sibling."

Ty shrugged. "I never was much for standing in the shadows."

At the thought of a younger Ty daring twice as much to keep up with his gifted older brother, Eleanor smiled. "I thought that about you."

The corner of Ty's mouth lifted. "What about you? Must never have been boring growing up with Senator Cole Aston as a father."

"No, I can't say I was ever bored." Just never quite part of the family. "He is constantly into something."

"Like donating the money to open the new hospital wing?"

"That's one of the few things he's done that makes me very proud to be an Aston."

"The few?"

She shrugged. "He's a politician. He does what he needs to do to get votes. My whole life was planned around what would help Daddy most in the polls."

Ty regarded her for long enough that Eleanor wanted to squirm, but didn't.

He leaned back in his chair, eyed her curiously with a glimmer of bedevilment dancing in his eyes. "Tell me, Eleanor. Come election day, do you vote for dear old dad?"

Her jaw dropped. Never had anyone asked her that. They just assumed…

"I'd answer that," she began, keeping her tone even, "but then I'd have to kill you. So I'm just going to plead the Fifth."

Ty burst out laughing. "Like I said, you're funny. I like you, Ellie."

Yeah, she liked him, too.

Except for the nickname, which she could do without, although there was something about the way it rolled off his tongue that was starting to get to her.

She only hoped that later down the road liking Ty didn't come back to haunt her.

CHAPTER FIVE

ELEANOR HAD SEEN Ty several times around the hospital, had even grabbed a few quick cups of coffee with him in the cafeteria and twice they'd shared lunch.

She'd heard the rumors that were flying around, had fiercely denied them, but everyone knew Ty's reputation.

"Just be careful, Eleanor," Linda Busby, a registered nurse in her early sixties who worked in the NICU, warned. "Dr. Donaldson is wonderful. I swear every woman he's gone out with still sings his praises, so I know he's a great guy. However, you don't play the dating games most men and women do, and I don't want to see you get hurt."

"We're just friends." They were. Not once had Ty attempted to kiss her or hold her hand other than the brief moment at the restaurant. Actually, on the night of the ribbon-cutting he'd touched her more than he had all the other times they'd seen each other since then combined.

"Watch him," Linda warned, her hands on her hips. "He isn't known for being just friends with pretty young girls."

Seeing Ty behind the nurse and knowing her friend was unaware of their eavesdropper, who was nodding his head in agreement with everything Linda said, Eleanor bit back a smile.

"Then you might want to watch out for him, too. I hear he's into the whole cougar thing."

Linda spun at Ty's teasing comment, her face turning beet-red. She playfully smacked his arm. "You, young man, are bad."

His grin killed any argument anyone tried to make to the contrary. "Wanna be bad with me, darlin'?"

Linda shook her head, turned to Eleanor. "Like I said, watch this one. He uses that good-ole-boy Southern charm to boil our Northern-girl blood. You'd be wise to steer clear."

"You know you love me," Ty teased her.

Linda and Eleanor both rolled their eyes, making Ty laugh out loud.

"I've got work to do." She gave Ty a well-meaning glare and pointed her finger at him. "You behave."

"Yes, ma'am." He gave her his lopsided grin.

Linda walked away smiling, shaking her head and mumbling something about God having blessed Texas.

"You here to check on the new twenty-four-week preemie?" Eleanor asked him, wondering why her heart was beating so fast in her chest just from Ty being near.

His expression sobered. "I am. The family given him a name yet?"

She'd taken a peek at the newborn herself just a few minutes prior to Linda giving her advice about spending so much time with Ty.

"No." Eleanor shook her head, walking with him to the little boy's incubator. "He's just Male Griffin at the moment. Linda told me they say they aren't going to. They think that will only make them get more attached."

Glancing toward her, Ty winced. "They've not been to see him?"

"The father has, but he refuses to let his wife come. Her nurse says she asks continually but that she won't go against her husband's wishes."

His eyes assessing the tiny baby he'd watched be born and had immediately taken charge of, Ty sighed. "He's trying to protect her, but how is she not supposed to already be attached to a baby she carried inside her body for twenty-four weeks and built a lifetime of dreams around?"

"He knows her better than we do, but if she wants to see her baby, he shouldn't keep her from doing so. If he dies and she hasn't seen him even though she really wanted to, she may never forgive herself."

"Exactly my thoughts," Ty agreed.

Eleanor couldn't imagine the fear the baby's parents must be going through, the worries, the doubts. Her heart went out both to the parents and to the little boy who very well might not live.

Ty examined the baby, discussed his immediate care with Eleanor, asking her opinion on a few points and then they stood next to the incubator, watching the baby struggle for each second of life, alive only by the technology that kept him that way.

Even though she dealt with similar cases routinely, just looking at the tiny baby was enough to make Eleanor's heart clench.

As if maybe he'd had a few heart clenches of his own, Ty inhaled sharply, then turned toward her. "Pick you up at six for the fund-raiser tonight, right?"

Her pulse jumping for no good reason at all except for the way his gaze held hers, Eleanor shook her head. "My father insists on sending his limo for you."

Ty's dark brows drew together. "Will you already be in that limo?"

Eleanor shrugged. "I have no idea what order my father has planned. I thought perhaps you two had discussed the arrangements." She'd barely spoken to her father since the morning he'd summoned Ty to the Aston penthouse. "I just know that when he called me this morning he insisted on providing our transportation. For us both to be ready so we wouldn't be late arrivals. He wants us to make a big media splash."

Apparently her father planned to milk her having a date for all it was worth. Just the thought of being in the crowded ballroom, of all the back-slapping and paparazzi that would be there was enough to make her heart do that funny little flipping sensation that always preceded a full-blown panic attack. She hated crowds, hated that as the senator's daughter she'd be photographed. At least tonight she'd have Ty at her side. Perhaps for that she should thank her father because she couldn't have made it through the ribbon-cutting without him.

Ty's lips twisted with displeasure. "For future reference, I need to let your father know that I prefer to pick up my own dates."

Future dates? As in dates her father arranged between them? Or real dates? As in dates that he asked her to go on with him because he wanted to be with her?

Better yet, why did she desperately wish tonight was a real date?

Ty supposed there were advantages to arriving to pick Eleanor up from her apartment in the Aston limo. For instance, he didn't have to find parking while he ran inside to collect her.

Although a nice apartment complex, Eleanor didn't live in the grandiose style of the Aston penthouse. Not that he actually saw the inside of her apartment. The doorman buzzed her and she insisted on meeting him in the lobby. Fine, nothing was going according to how he'd pictured it in his mind.

He'd look a dork for bringing flowers and handing them to her in the lobby, but so be it because he'd wanted to do this right. Whatever right was.

The moment his gaze landed on her stepping out of the elevator he felt like a country hick come to the big city and about to meet a glamorous star.

"Hello, Ellie," he greeted her in a worshipful whisper.

Her forehead creased. "I told you not to call me that."

"And I agreed to only do so when you stole my breath, darlin'."

She reached out, placed her palm near his nostrils. "Still breathing, so don't let it happen again."

But her demand was tempered by the way her eyes had lit up when he'd reminded her of their deal.

"You are beautiful, by the way," he added, thinking truer words had never been spoken. She'd clipped her hair up, but much looser than she wore for work. Although her dress was much more demure than the red number she'd worn for the ribbon-cutting, she still looked supersexy in the silky black number clinging to her body.

"So are you."

At her response, Ty glanced down at his tuxedo. A black-and-white penguin suit when he was more comfortable in scrubs or a pair of well-worn jeans. Nothing beautiful about him. But Eleanor was truly gorgeous. She looked as if she should be gracing an ad for a classic movie much as Audrey Hepburn would have or Grace Kelly. Eleanor shamed them both.

"Nice flowers." She smiled softly at him when he just stood staring at her.

Wondering at how his chest tightened at her shy smile, Ty grinned back. "Yeah, darlin', I think your doorman has a thing for me. He insisted I take these..." he held up the bouquet "...although I'm pretty sure he stole them out of one of the floral arrangements in here." He held them out toward her. "You better stash them in your apartment to save me from getting in trouble, just in case."

She took the flowers, closed her eyes and breathed in their fragrance, then smiled in a way that really put his chest into lockdown. "Thank you, Ty, but you didn't have to bring me flowers. It's not as if this is a real date."

Not a real date? Hadn't they already been through this the night they'd gone to dinner?

"What is it, then?"

Cheeks pink, her gaze averted. "A deal you and my father arranged."

Was that how she saw tonight? As something he and her father had arranged? Did she not want to be with him? He'd thought… Never mind what he'd thought.

"I still think you should have just asked one of your women to go with you to Texas. You'd have saved yourself a lot of trouble." She walked over to the front desk, gave the flowers to the smiling older man there, leaned over and kissed his cheek.

When she returned to where he stood watching, Ty scratched his head. "My women?"

"One of the women you've taken out for real."

Enough was enough. "This is real."

Not responding, she just smiled as if she was humoring him. She probably was.

"Come on, darlin'," he said, not liking the frustration moving through him. He took her hand. "Let's go get the party started. For real."

Eleanor laughed at Ty's latest corny joke. He'd been telling her silly little jokes all night. If she found herself feeling panicky or uptight, he'd lean over and whisper something totally outlandish in her ear just for her to hear.

"You're beautiful.

"You're one sexy woman, darlin'.

"I'm the luckiest man at the fund-raiser because I'm with you.

"Just in case there's any doubt, let me remind you. This is a real date."

Champagne had been flowing freely at her father's announcement that he planned to run for another senate term. As if anyone had thought otherwise. Eleanor needed to have stopped drinking prior to her last glass of bubbly because her insides felt a little too warm and cozy. Because Ty's whispered words were starting to get to her, were starting to make her want to do some whispering back into his ear.

Things like, "You're gorgeous, Ty," and "You're one sexy man, darling," and "I'm the luckiest woman at the fund-raiser because I'm with you." And "I'm so glad this is a real date, because I'd really like you to kiss me before the night is over."

"Wow!" he exclaimed, drawing her attention away from her daydreaming. "That's your sister? The papers don't do her justice."

Ty's words pulled Eleanor right out of her dreamy euphoria. Here they went. How many times throughout her life had she been interested in someone only to have them meet Brooke and forget she even existed? How many times had she been used as a means to get an introduction to glorious, glamorous Brooke?

"You want me to introduce you?"

Her words must have tipped him off, because he shifted, dragged his eyes away from Brooke and looked fully at Eleanor, searching her eyes.

She didn't look away, didn't back down.

For once she wasn't going to be all nice about

a man who was with her but wanted Brooke instead.

"Only if you want to, Ellie. Only if you want to."

She gritted her teeth. The nickname only served to remind her of the contrast between her and her sister. Forever she'd be Jelly Ellie when put next to beauty-queen Brooke.

"Oh, yes, I want to. Let's go." Might as well get it over with. Probably, if the truth be told, an introduction to Brooke had been on his agenda all along. Didn't he realize all he'd have had to do was mention to the senator that he preferred slender blondes and Cole would have had him taking Brooke to Texas instead?

Brooke held court in the midst of about twenty people, mostly besotted men. She barely paid any heed to Eleanor joining her. Until her gaze landed on Ty.

"You brought Dr. Yummy to meet me." Brooke's gaze ran suggestively over Ty. "Goody."

Goody, indeed. Eleanor wanted to gag. Why was she doing this? She liked Ty. Really liked him. Why was she serving him on a silver platter to her silly, immature sister?

Better to get it over with now than to get her emotions more entangled and then discover she had just been a means to get to her sister.

She already knew how that felt.

"Actually, it's Dr. Donaldson," Ty smoothly corrected with an easy smile. He slid his arm around Eleanor's waist, his hand resting possessively at her lower back. "But as I'm your sister's date for the evening, you can call me Ty."

"As in tie me up and tie me down?" Brooke flirted, still eyeing Ty and making no pretense that she was interested.

Gag. Gag. Gag. Did men really find that attractive?

Looking at her sister in her figure-hugging blue dress and flawless appearance, Eleanor decided that if you looked like Brooke men would overlook almost everything. And did.

But rather than respond to Brooke's obvious interest, Ty lifted Eleanor's hand to his lips, pressed a kiss to her fingertips and winked at her. "Only if Ellie is the one doing the tying."

It was a toss-up as to which sister's jaw hit the floor first.

"Pardon?" Brooke blinked, sure she'd misunderstood, glancing back and forth between him and Eleanor.

Eleanor couldn't speak. Had Ty really just dissed her sister in favor of *her?* In public? Had he gone mad?

"Sure thing." Ty smoothly misunderstood Brooke's comment, whether feigned or real Eleanor wasn't sure. "We were headed to the dance floor anyway. Nice to meet any family member of Ellie's."

His hand stayed low on Eleanor's back, guiding her toward the dance floor. She was too blown away to put up any kind of argument, instead instinctively wrapping her arms around his neck.

Ty's arms settled around her and they swayed in time to the music. "She always like that?"

Wondering at how their bodies had so naturally fallen into rhythm together, at how he had just done something no man ever had—chosen to spend time with her rather than Brooke—Eleanor shook her head.

Maybe she really had drunk more champagne than she'd realized. Maybe she was so drunk that she'd imagined everything that had just happened. Maybe she was really passed out on the ladies' room floor.

"No?"

Automatically, she opened her mouth to defend her sister. It was what she'd done her whole life. But when her gaze met Ty's she found the truth spilling from her mouth. "Usually she's worse." Oh, yeah, she'd drunk one glass of champagne too many. "Although really it's not her fault." Old habits died hard. "Everyone spoils her so it's only natural that she expects everyone to bow at her feet." Eleanor shrugged. "They usually do."

Holding her close, Ty shuddered. "Tell me you took after your mother."

All too aware of the strong arms around her, of the muscular body against hers, of the wonderfully male scent filling her nostrils, Eleanor laughed. "Because my mother is the only immediate family member you've not met and maybe there's hope yet?"

His husky laugh warmed her insides. "Always knew you were one sharp cookie, Ellie."

"I wouldn't hold my breath if I were you because she's here and no doubt you'll meet her before the night is through. I saw the senator and her looking our way earlier. And do not call me that name."

"Don't glare at me, *Ellie*." His lips twitched. "I'm just keeping to our deal."

"You've called me Ellie four times in the past five minutes," she pointed out, frustrated at his insistence on the name. Sure, the way it rolled off his tongue always made her breath catch, but she didn't like the name.

"Exactly."

His one word sliced right through the past. She couldn't look away from the sincerity in his eyes. Ty found her attractive, had chosen her over Brooke—something that she'd never dreamed would happen—and he was holding her close to his body.

His wonderful, warm, hard, fantastic-smelling body that was obviously affected by holding her close.

"You are a very beautiful woman, Ellie Aston, and you have taken my breath away from the moment I arrived to pick you up this evening."

Eleanor's insides melted to ooey-gooey feminine happiness and for once she didn't even glare at him for using the nickname she despised.

After all, a deal was a deal.

"When you look at me like that you make me feel beautiful," she admitted, wondering if she was a fool for revealing so much, wondering if perhaps she should have cut off the champagne long ago because he couldn't really be looking at her that way. Could he?

His fingers lifted her chin. He studied her face, her eyes, until she wanted to squirm away. He leaned forward and pressed the gentlest of kisses to her forehead. So soft she could almost think he was hesitant, but he wasn't. He was strong and confident. His kiss had revered her as if she were something fragile, precious.

How would it feel to kiss Ty for real? On the mouth? To have him enthralled in passion, touching her, kissing her as if he craved her lips more than the air he breathed?

His hand pressed against her back, holding her close to him. Her cheek rested against his chest. She breathed in his musky fragrance, the smell of him intoxicating her much more than any alcohol she'd consumed.

He bent, spoke close to her ear. "I want to kiss you, Ellie, but not here. Not with all the photographers. I want our first kiss to be just between us, not fodder for some gossip page."

She wanted to be kissed. Desperately. By Ty. She wanted that first kiss. Thousands more.

"We can leave anytime," she offered.

He leaned back enough to look her in the eyes, as if trying to decide exactly what she was saying.

"Now," she clarified. "Let's leave now."

"Oh, yeah."

Hand in hand, they headed out of the ballroom, through the glitzy foyer, got their coats. Ty helped her into hers then they walked out onto the sidewalk.

As soon as Eleanor finished asking the attendant to call for the limo, Ty lifted her hand to his lips.

"Thank you for tonight, darlin'."

The brisk night air grasped at her and she shivered. Reality began to set in, to wash away the effects of the alcohol haze that had enveloped her. Self-doubt set in.

"You don't have to do that, you know," she told him. "You've more than done your duty."

His eyes darkened. "Done my duty?"

"As my escort for the evening. You were wonderful."

"If I hadn't wanted to come with you tonight, darlin', I wouldn't have." His eyes glittered. "I'm here because I want to be. Because this was a date. A real date."

Had he drunk so much that he'd fallen into the same fantasy as she had?

"My father is a very persuasive man. Maybe you just think you want to be here."

"What? He used some kind of super-politician force to trick me into thinking I wanted to spend my evening with his lovely daughter?" Ty shook his head, blew a puff of cold breath into his hands, then smiled wickedly at her. "I don't think so. We Texans are made of stronger stuff. I'm here because I want to be with you. No other reason."

Eleanor blushed. "Thank you."

"No. Thank you, Ellie." Then he surprised her by pulling her to him. He kissed her fully on the mouth despite the fact they stood on the street and Lord only knew who might see them.

She didn't care. Later she might, but at the moment all that mattered was that he was kissing her. Finally.

His lips were firm, confident, sure in their movements over hers. He tasted of heaven. He tasted of fire.

She wanted more. Much more.

Her fingers wove into the hair at his nape. Soft strands with just a touch of curl. She'd done so throughout the evening while dancing, but now she latched on, clasping the locks tightly within her grasp, needing him closer and closer still.

Vaguely she was aware of the limousine pulling up to the curb, of her and Ty separating long enough for him to generously tip the attendant and to help her into the back of the car.

Then he joined her and she was back where she wanted to be.

In Ty Donaldson's arms.

Ty moved in a blur. A desire-driven blur.

One spurred on by a woman he foolishly hadn't realized capable of such passion.

Ellie had passion.

He pressed his lips to her throat just so, and she moaned, spurring him on. He traced his hands down her body, touching places he'd carefully avoided while holding her on the dance floor.

"You are so hot," he breathed against her throat, caressing his way to the sweet indention at her clavicle.

"Because you're touching me," she answered

in a husky tone, her fingers threading through his hair, holding him to her. "That makes me feel hot."

Somehow they made it into his apartment still dressed.

Once he closed the door and secured the lock, he made haste with her dress, letting it drop somewhere on the way to his bedroom.

He pushed her back onto his bed, loving how she looked lying there, watching him as he stripped off his clothes in record time.

"Wow," she breathed, reaching her hand up to run over his abs. "You're perfect, Ty."

"You're what's perfect," he corrected, joining her on the bed and pressing his body against hers. "So very perfect. See how you fit against me? Perfect."

Her mouth and hands were all over him, leaving trails of goose bumps, making waves through his nervous system, rewriting his definition of pleasure.

Pushing her bra aside, he closed his lips around

one pert nipple, then the other, taking turns laving her until she arched off the bed.

"Ty." Her fingers cradled his head. He suckled harder, taking great pleasure in her breasts, in her passionate responses to his every touch.

"Tell me what you want, Ellie," he encouraged, wanting to give her every pleasure, wanting to give her everything within his power to give. "Tell me where to touch you, how you want to be touched."

For the briefest moment she stiffened in his embrace, her eyes searching his, then she relaxed and guided his mouth to hers.

She kissed him long, hard, deep, leaving him breathless.

"I. Want. You."

He wanted her, too. He was pretty sure he told her somewhere during the time he stripped off her panties and then his boxers.

The way Eleanor's eyes ate up his bare flesh set him afire, made him ache for her touch, for her body.

She looked at him as if she couldn't wait another moment to feel him against her. To feel him inside her.

Maybe she couldn't because she tugged on his shoulders, pulling him to her and wrapping her delectable legs around his.

Hands were everywhere.

Mouths were everywhere.

They touched desperately.

They touched with need, committing each other's bodies to memory, learning every nuance, lighting fires that burned wickedly hot.

When Ty couldn't stand another moment, he thrust deep between her welcoming thighs, plunging into almost blinding pleasure, knowing she'd rewritten much more than his definition of pleasure.

Ellie's cry of satisfaction was everything.

CHAPTER SIX

WHAT HAD SHE DONE?

Not that Eleanor didn't know.

She'd spent the night in Ty Donaldson's bed. Now she knew exactly why all his exes smiled and thought he was the most awesome thing ever.

He was.

Wow.

She rolled over and looked at his sleeping form lit by the streaks of early-morning light. He was beautiful. Truly deep-down beautiful. One of God's loveliest creations.

She wanted to reach out and touch him, to stroke her finger over the strong planes of his cheek, to feel the soft wisps of his hair, to feel the full softness of his lips. But she kept her hands to herself.

She wouldn't risk waking him. No way did

she want to see the disappointment that would dawn in his eyes when he realized what they'd done, who he'd spent his night with.

Then again, spending the night with a woman was no big deal for Ty. Just because it was something she never did, it didn't make their night out of the ordinary for him.

To Ty, she was just another of a long string of women he'd made love to.

Had sex with.

Sure, with the way his hands and mouth had worshipped her body, she'd felt like she'd been made love to. But she wasn't so naive as to not realize the truth.

Somehow she managed to get out of the bed without waking him. Desperate for a fast escape, she snatched a pair of way-too-big drawstring running shorts and a T-shirt from the floor, gathered her gown and clothing.

Her heart pounded faster, harder. So loud she couldn't believe Ty didn't wake. Maybe he only faked sleep because he didn't want to face her any more than she wanted to face him. Maybe he wished she'd hurry and get out of his apartment.

The muscles in her chest tightened, squeezing her rib cage almost painfully. Her hands sweated so badly that she almost dropped her clothes.

She sucked in one last breath, storing the vision of the sheet draped low on his waist to memory, knowing that seeing him like this, his beautiful body relaxed and completely loved by her, would never happen again.

Buzz. Buzz. Buzz.

Oh, hell! Her heart pounding, Eleanor desperately dug in her purse for her cell phone, which was obviously still on vibration only. In the silence of the room the buzz sounded as if it should register on the Richter scale. She almost clicked the phone silent, then realized that the only calls she ever got in the early-morning hours were emergency calls. Her heart pounded all the harder.

"No need to leave the room," a sleepy-sounding Ty drawled from behind her, causing her to freeze halfway to the door. "I'm awake."

Eleanor's pulse thrummed in her ears as she answered and listened to the caller. "I'll be right there."

She clicked her cell phone off. Taking a deep breath, she slowly turned to face him, dreading whatever she might see on his face in the early-morning light.

"Mornin', darlin'," he surprised her by drawling, his gaze taking her in as he scooted up in the bed. The bedsheet rode even lower on his hips, barely covering his impressive bottom half. His very impressive upper half shamed the six-pack fantasy she'd had of him. He patted the bed, motioning for her to climb in next to him. "From your end of the conversation, I figure that was the hospital. Before you go, give me a proper good- morning kiss."

A proper good-morning kiss? As if she even knew what that was.

In her mind, she tossed everything she held on the floor and dived back into bed with him, smashed her lips to his, rubbed her body all over his until he gave her a proper good-morning everything.

But, um, she couldn't do that.

So she cleared her throat and wished like crazy that she'd not lingered quite so long taking in how beautiful he was. Whereas he was gorgeous in the early-morning light, she imagined her hair was wild, her eyes puffy from lack of sleep, makeup smudged from not having been removed, and how sexy could she possibly be standing there in his too-big clothes?

She was just plain, ordinary Eleanor Aston, nothing like the glamorous women he was used to who probably gave him glorious mornings-after.

Breathing got more and more difficult. Her palms grew more and more clammy.

Oh, yeah, she really just wanted to click her heels together and be far, far away from Ty Donaldson and all memories of the night they'd shared.

Ty stretched his arms over his head, enjoying the light ache in his muscles from the night's activities.

The night's very enjoyable, rather vigorous activities with the siren standing in his bedroom.

Wearing his gym shorts and T-shirt.

Holding her dress, shoes, purse and phone.

Looking like a deer caught in headlights.

The happiness within him dwindled.

"You were leaving, weren't you?"

Her wide eyes and guilty face answered before her stuttering lips did. "I—I need to go to the hospital."

He shook his head, anger replacing every good feeling he'd awakened with. "Really? You were just going to sneak out without so much as 'Thank you, Ty'?"

"I…" She glanced down, took a deep breath. "Thank you, Ty."

His jaw clenched. "For?"

She shrugged. "What is it you want me to say?"

That she'd enjoyed last night as much as he had. That she hadn't been going to creep out of his apartment without waking him. That what she'd really like was a repetition of how they'd spent the night, that she'd felt all the things he had.

Because even as angry as he was, just looking at her, at seeing how his T-shirt stretched over those amazing breasts of hers, at seeing the long span of her legs beneath his running shorts, he wanted her. Wanted to pull her back into the bed beside him and kiss her until she was breathless, make love to her until she cried out his name and begged him for more.

Until sneaking out of his house while he slept off the effects of their night together would be the last thing she'd ever consider doing.

He ran his hands through his hair, took a deep breath. "Ellie."

Her weight shifted, drawing his attention to her bare feet. He'd kissed those feet, massaged them and worked his way up her calves and…

"Look, Ty," she began, wincing when his gaze lifted to hers. "I—I have to get to the hospital. One of my patients coded and they couldn't revive her. The family wasn't there, but they've been called and asked to come to the hospital. I need to be the one to tell them."

Ty nodded. As frustrating as he found her leaving without them talking, he understood. He'd feel the same.

As if his thought conjured a call of his own, Ty's phone rang. The hospital. If not for the seriousness that would have prompted the call, he'd have laughed.

He took the call then clicked off his phone.

"There's been a multicar wreck in one of the tunnels. Multiple injuries, at least two of which are infants and another's a pregnant woman. Looks as if you aren't the only one who has to head to the hospital. Let me grab some scrubs for both of us and we'll share a cab."

Eleanor stepped to the curb as the taxi Ty had hailed came to a screeching halt.

He opened the cab door and waited for her to step in. He'd barely said two words to her since he'd gotten out of bed and grabbed clothes for them both. He was upset that she'd been going to leave without waking him. What had he expected? That she'd snuggle up next to him as if they were longtime lovers? Or that she'd awaken him with kisses and promises of an early-morning repeat?

Was that what he was used to?

"Where to?" the driver asked, eyeing the heels and gown Eleanor carried then letting his midnight gaze travel over the baggy scrubs she wore. With the drawstring waist they weren't too bad and she'd rolled up their long legs to make them work.

Without meeting the driver's gaze, because Lord knew he had to know how she'd spent her night, she spat out the hospital's address.

Ty slid into the backseat next to her.

The cab smelled of years of use badly disguised with an air freshener hanging from the rearview mirror.

So how in the world was it that the one scent that stood out in her mind was that of the man next to her? A scent that filled her mind with memories of the night before.

"You okay, darlin'?"

"Fine," she answered, without glancing toward him. Really, what was she supposed to say? That this was awkward and that, yes, she'd kissed him all over the night before but now she didn't know what to say to him and would like to crawl under the seat?

At least she hadn't stuttered.

Eleanor couldn't keep her eyes from watering as she sat across from the young couple on the sofa. The young couple to whom she'd just delivered devastating news.

"Did she...?" The young woman's head bowed, then her tear-filled eyes lifted to Eleanor. "Did she suffer?"

Shaking her head, Eleanor reached over and took the woman's hand. "No. She died in her sleep."

The baby's body just hadn't been strong enough to maintain life outside her mother's body. She'd lived a week, but only with the aid of the respirator and numerous other machines performing the bodily functions her tiny underdeveloped body hadn't been able to.

"I should have been here," the woman said between tears. "I shouldn't have left the hospital."

"Your family wasn't wrong to want you to go home to get a good night's sleep. Your body is recovering and needs rest," Eleanor assured her, squeezing the woman's hand. Her poor husband had his arm around her but looked as if he was about to burst into tears himself at any moment.

Eleanor spent a few more minutes with the couple then left the room to give them a few minutes of privacy. And to collect her own emotions.

Because she was a mess.

Losing one of her patients always tore her heart to bits, but her heart had already been in tatters before she'd even gotten to the hospital.

"There you are," Ty said from right behind her.

She faced him, couldn't help but immediately be struck with the memories of what they'd done only hours before.

"You okay, darlin'?" he asked, looking and sounding the same as he always did. Like handsome, charming Dr. Tyler Donaldson. Because for Ty last night hadn't been anything out of the ordinary. But he'd probably rightly assumed that for her last night had been extraordinary.

Which was why she had to save face, to pretend she hadn't seen stars when he'd made her orgasm, to pretend that last night hadn't been the best time of her life.

Ha. As if she had that many comparisons. A quickie during her freshman year at college with a short-term boyfriend. Short-term meaning he'd dumped her immediately after their one and only time together.

No way was she letting Ty Donaldson do the same. Not when she had to work with him. Already she'd had to field questions from Scarlet and several other coworkers who'd seen photographs of her and Ty in the society pages. The last thing she wanted was her friends and colleagues to feel sorry for her.

"Of course I'm okay." Which sounded great,

but she couldn't bring herself to look into those gorgeous eyes, neither could she prevent the heat burning her face. "Why wouldn't I be?"

His expression tightened. "You just left the family, right? The family of your morning code?"

Eleanor fought putting her hands over her face in shame. He'd been talking about work and she'd been… "Yes. You're right. I—I…"

Oh, please, don't let the stuttering start. He'd know how nervous she was.

He raked his fingers through his hair, glanced around the unit, then for once seemed at a loss. When his gaze met hers, the fatigue she hadn't seen earlier was etched on his handsome face. "I have an emergency C-section that came in this morning. Twins. The pediatrician for the second baby's team isn't here yet. Go in with me in case there are complications?"

Despite the fact that being anywhere near him was the last thing she wanted, she couldn't refuse. Not when a baby's life might be on the line. "Sure."

In silence they scrubbed and went into the obstetrics surgery room specially designated for preemies. Every second that ticked by, Eleanor felt more and more awkward, more and more as if the nurses must be able to look at her and Ty and know what they'd done.

The first baby was delivered without any major birthing complications, but his Apgar score was only a seven. Ty assessed the baby, cleared his throat and examined him all in a matter of seconds.

Watching him work, Eleanor couldn't help but admire his skill, his finesse, the way his big hands were so gentle as they handled the baby. Just as they'd been so gentle when they'd touched her.

He was a gentle man and she hadn't been anything special, just the result of too much champagne and the next notch on his belt. Nothing more.

She closed her eyes, forcing her thoughts from her mind. When she opened them, her gaze immediately collided with Ty's. He stared at her for a brief moment as if trying to read her thoughts, then that sexy crooked grin of his slid into place as a peace offering of sorts.

But Eleanor couldn't smile back.

She just couldn't. Sure, the sight of his generous mouth curved upward made her want to smile back. Instead, she hardened her resolve. He might be used to women thinking he was amazing after a night of his loving, but she needed distance to survive emotionally.

Ty's smile waned. A nurse spoke to him, pulling his attention away from where he still looked at Eleanor as if he wanted to probe inside her head.

The second baby, another boy, made his entrance into the world. Eleanor focused her attention on the newborn, giving him a thorough once-over and realizing his lungs weren't as developed as his brother's.

Telling the nurse her intentions, she gave the baby a few breaths with a manual respirator, hoping to stimulate his lungs, but was unsuccessful in her efforts.

"You want me to intubate him?" Ty asked from beside her. He was so close she could feel his body heat. If she leaned just a little she'd brush against his arm.

"I can do it," she assured him, having done it many times previously and wondering why he'd offered, wondering why she so desperately wanted to lean into him.

"I'm sure you can. Just wanted to help you."

"This is my job," she reminded him. "I'm good at what I do, Dr. Donaldson, but thanks for the offer."

The nurse assisting Eleanor glanced back and forth between them and Eleanor fought against blushing.

She threaded the tiny tube through the baby's nostril, checked placement, then secured the line. She turned to where Ty stood, but he was no longer there. She supposed he'd gone with his team to the NICU, but surprisingly she'd not been aware when he'd walked away.

Good, the less aware she was of the man, the better.

* * *

"I know you've had a crazy morning with the code, then talking with the family, then working the trauma delivery with Dr. Donaldson, but you are extraordinarily quiet this morning." Linda stepped up beside Eleanor while she examined a thirty-two-week preemie who was now a month old and would be going home within a week if all continued to progress well. "The fund-raiser for your dad run late last evening?"

Frustrated at the recurrent reminders of the night before, Eleanor thought she might scream. She straightened from examining the baby. "How is it that everyone knows where I spent my evening?"

Lord, she hoped they didn't know where she'd spent her night.

Staring at her a little too closely, Linda's brow arched high. "Should I assume that you didn't attend your father's fund-raiser ball, then?"

Sighing with frustration and remorse that she'd snapped at her coworker, Eleanor stroked her fingertip over the tiny baby's precious cheek, loving how his reflexes kicked in and he turned in the direction she'd touched. Developing reflexes was a sign of progress, of increased survival chances.

"No, sorry, you're right," she relented, knowing that she was being overly sensitive, that she just wanted this crazy day to end, and it wasn't even noon yet. "I was there."

"It's not like you to be cranky." Linda's eyes were way too astute. "Things didn't go well?"

"Things went just fine." Hoping she would take the hint, Eleanor made a fuss of continuing to check the little boy, talking to him softly as she did so.

"Dr. Donaldson came, too?"

Oh, he came all right.

Eleanor winced at her crude thought. Her very inappropriate thought. She knew she shouldn't have reacted, that Linda was too keen to have missed the telltale expression.

"Let's not talk about him, okay?" she settled with saying. "I want to know about Rochelle. How is she?"

"She's holding her own." Linda paused for effect, then continued, "You should probably know that he was looking for you after he finished up with the twin."

Eleanor fought to keep from sucking in air. "Maybe he wanted an update on the other twin or something."

"Or something," Linda mumbled as she walked away from the incubator, shaking her head as she went.

Turning back to assess the baby, Eleanor bit her lower lip. What was Ty thinking? Was he relieved that what he probably considered the worst mistake of his life wasn't making a fuss?

She finished examining the baby, entered her notes into the computer, thoroughly cleansed her hands, then moved on to her next little patient.

But before she started, she spotted Ty entering the unit. Her breath caught. The man was way too beautiful. Tall, dark, handsome, fantastic in bed.

A flashback of her naked body tangled with his flashed through her head. Images of their bodies molded together, gyrating, thrusting, exploding. How was she ever going to look at Ty without remembering? Without thinking of all the marvelous ways he'd touched her body?

He headed straight for her and although she might have tried had she thought she'd be successful, there was no place for her to hide.

"We need to talk about what happened last night."

Hoping no one was close enough to overhear their conversation, she glanced around the nursery. No one seemed to be paying them the slightest attention, but looks could be deceiving.

"Can't we talk about this later?" She really didn't want to talk about it at all. She just wanted to forget.

"Tonight?"

She shook her head. "I'm busy."

Ty's face clouded. "All night? Or you just don't want to spend the evening with me?"

"I have plans." Did reading the latest medical journal and going to the gym count?

His lips pursed. "Cancel them. We need to discuss what happened last night."

Knowing they had to be attracting attention, even if only Linda's, she glanced around the room again. "No, we don't, and especially not here."

Seeming to recall where they were, he glanced around, sighed. "Fine, then go out with me tonight so we can talk somewhere that's not here."

"No." She couldn't risk going out with him again. She wasn't that strong, might end up begging him to kiss her, touch her, take her to heights previously unknown. "But if you insist on having this conversation right now, let's at least go somewhere private."

"You have time for a coffee?"

If it got them away from the prying eyes and ears of their coworkers then she'd make time.

"If we make it quick." She glanced at her watch as if she was doing him a favor by agreeing. At least, she hoped that's how it came across. Every instinct within her told her to not let Ty know how he'd blown her away the night before, to protect herself. "Let me finish my assessment and I'll be right with you."

Hands shaking, heart thumping, blood raging through her vessels, she examined the baby, entered in her notes and new orders, then headed out of the NICU. For coffee.

With the man she'd touched all over with her mouth.

With the man who'd touched her all over with his mouth.

Best she forget. He probably wanted to take her out so he could make sure she knew last night meant nothing.

"Or something," Linda reminded her of her earlier comment with a grin when Eleanor walked by the smug nurse.

Eleanor's face flamed, but she kept walking, not meeting her coworker's eyes.

Yeah, the sooner she got the coffee break over with the sooner she could forget the previous night had happened.

At least, she hoped she could forget.

* * *

Ty ordered two coffees, grabbed a couple of sweetener packets and cream and sat down at a table.

"Hey, Dr. Donaldson," a cute little brunette from the surgical floor greeted him, stopping at his table and smiling prettily at him. "You want some company?"

Automatically he grinned at the woman, but he shook his head. He gestured to the second cup of coffee. "I'm meeting Dr. Aston."

Looking disappointed, the woman nodded as if she understood. "Maybe next time."

Although usually he would have flirted back with her as naturally as taking his next breath, Ty didn't say anything, just stirred sugar into his steaming cup of coffee. He hadn't even called her darlin'. What was up with that?

"We can do this later if need be."

He glanced up and knew exactly what was up. Ellie and the night they'd spent together. The amazing, out-of-this-world night they'd spent together.

Her face was red, her gaze wouldn't meet his and she sounded agitated. A new wave of frustration hit him.

"Why would we need to do that?" He took a deep breath, reminded himself that patience was a virtue even if his had felt in short supply from the moment he'd awakened and realized she was skipping out on him.

She gestured in the direction of the departing woman.

He pulled out the chair next to his. "Have a seat."

She sat. Not in the chair next to his but in the one directly opposite. He almost laughed at her bullheadedness. Any moment he expected her to cross her arms and glare at him in her stereotypical fashion.

If he knew what the hell he'd done to deserve her antagonism, it would be one thing, but as best he could recall, the night had been amazing all the way around.

With care, he slid the cup of coffee across to

her along with two packets of sweetener and one cream.

Surprise flickered across her face. "You know how I take my coffee?"

His lips twitched. "We've had coffee together several times over the past week. I pay attention to details."

She tore the packets of sweetener open and poured the contents into her cup. "You'll get no argument from me on that one."

"Meaning?"

She popped the top of the creamer, her face blazing red. "I'd think it obvious. You knew how I take my coffee so you must pay attention to details."

She made a production of stirring, then taking a sip. Ty had to force his gaze away from her mouth to keep from staring, to keep from remembering where that mouth had been during the night.

Why had she been leaving that morning without waking him? Why was she acting as if she was angry with him? Had she not felt the same things he had?

"About last night," he began, but she held up her hand.

"Don't worry about it." She took a slow sip of her coffee as if to stress her next point. "Last night was no big deal."

Ouch. He studied her pale face, trying to read her thoughts, but, as she had for most of the morning, she held her emotions in check. Her face was a blank slate.

"You're sure?" He wasn't. Every aspect of the night had felt like a very big deal. Like something new and wonderful.

"Positive." She set her coffee cup on the table, looked into his eyes, but quickly glanced away, toying with the empty sweetener packet papers. "We drank too much champagne and got caught up in the celebration."

Sounded feasible to him, except that nothing similar had ever happened before and he hadn't had that much champagne.

As he searched Eleanor's eyes, her claim didn't

feel right. Just as the blank expression on her face didn't feel right. Not after having seen her so alive just a few hours before. He wanted a glimpse of her smile, just to see if he'd imagined how his pulse reacted. He wanted to touch her to see if he'd imagined how his body responded to her skin against his.

"Okay, so we drank too much and got caught up in the moment." He didn't buy it, but he'd go with the flow for now. "You were leaving without waking me. Why?"

What was wrong with him? Mornings-after were no big deal. At least, they never had been before.

"If we hadn't gotten called in to the hospital, I would have made you breakfast," he added with a grin, but the gesture didn't feel natural.

Just as she hadn't in the delivery room, Eleanor didn't respond to his grin other than to get pink splotches on her otherwise pale face. "Is that what you usually do? Cook breakfast for your...guests?"

He had cooked breakfast for women before.

Several times. But never at his place. He didn't
have women at his apartment. Going to their
place kept things simpler. Easier to walk away
when it wasn't your place you were leaving. He
had brought Eleanor to his apartment, made love
to her in his bed and she'd been the one who'd
been going to walk away. He hadn't liked that
one bit.

Ty sighed. He'd had a great time the night before. Not just the sex, but the entire evening.
Truthfully, he wouldn't mind a repeat—several
repeats. Obviously, she wasn't of the same mind.
She'd seemed to enjoy herself well enough, but
maybe the champagne really had been why she'd
relaxed and smiled so freely at him.

It seemed she wasn't overjoyed that she'd spent
the night with him. Actually, she was acting as
if he'd been one big disappointment all the way
around.

That was a feeling he was all too familiar with.

Well, hell.

"Breakfast?" Ty downed the rest of his coffee in one gulp, not caring that the hot liquid

scorched his throat, then stood and answered her question. "Not always, but at least you got a cup of coffee out of the deal."

CHAPTER SEVEN

LEANING BACK IN her chair and staring at the computer screen, Eleanor brushed a loose hair away from her face. Her entire body ached with fatigue and she'd been fighting nausea all morning.

She'd been at the hospital since about 4:00 a.m. Not that she'd been sleeping much since the night she'd spent with Ty. Sleep evaded her and when she did finally drift into sleep, memories haunted her dreams.

She rubbed tight muscles in her neck and left shoulder, forcing herself to quit thinking about Ty yet again. She'd survived five weeks without him and she'd survive the rest of her life, too. She just needed to focus on one day at a time, focus on work.

Rochelle wasn't doing well. The tiny little girl

had taken a turn for the worse and nothing Eleanor did seemed to be making a difference.

She studied the baby's chart, looking for anything she might have missed, anything she could try that she hadn't tried already.

There wasn't a logical reason why Rochelle had taken a turn for the worse. The baby had been getting a little stronger each day and then she'd just stopped.

The baby's father hadn't been to see his tiny daughter, was still grieving the loss of his wife and couldn't bear becoming attached to a baby he felt certain wasn't going to live. Eleanor had called him, told him that she was concerned about Rochelle's sudden failure to thrive and that she wasn't sure if they were going to be able to turn the baby's prognosis around. She'd asked him to come to the hospital, but he hadn't made any false promises.

"I heard you were still here."

Eleanor's heart jerked, slamming hard against her rib cage. She hadn't heard Ty walk up to where she worked in the small, private dictation room.

"You not talking to me?"

Taking a deep breath, she glanced up from the computer screen she'd pretended to study to keep from looking at him. She wanted to look so badly it scared her. She wanted to throw herself into his arms. Perhaps never having been the center of all that sexy Texan charm would have been better.

"Sorry," she said slowly, thinking about each syllable in the hope of preventing a stutter. "Just thinking."

"About Rochelle?"

About anything and everything to keep from thinking about him. But she wasn't about to admit how much she'd missed him when he'd obviously not missed her, had obviously moved on with his life, with her not having made a speed bump's worth of difference.

So she told him about the tiny baby girl who she feared had taken a turn for the worse she wouldn't pull back from. "She's dropped weight over the past week."

Ty sank down in the chair next to hers, stretched out his long legs. "I thought she'd pull through. That she was going to be a success story."

He was so close. Close enough she could smell the spicy clean scent of him. Close enough that his body heat radiated toward her. Close enough that all she had to do was reach out to touch him, to feel his skin beneath her fingertips.

She swallowed. Hard. "Me, too."

In silence, he studied the baby's record. "You've done everything possible."

She knew that the very nature of what they did meant they wouldn't always be successful. "I just keep thinking I've missed something, but I can't figure out what."

"Maybe it's more who you've missed rather than what."

Her breath catching in her throat, her gaze jerked toward him. "I haven't missed you."

Much.

She'd missed him like crazy.

She'd relived every touch shared between Ty and herself, and had cried more tears than she cared to recall.

"Darlin', for the record, I was referring to Rochelle's father." The corner of Ty's mouth twitched, but she wasn't sure if it was with annoyance or an almost smile.

She felt his gaze on her, but she refused to meet his eyes. She just couldn't. "Oh."

"But since you've brought up the subject of missing me—"

"Perhaps you misunderstood," she interrupted, feeling sweat pop out on the back of her neck. "I said I hadn't missed you."

"Perhaps we should discuss just how much you haven't missed me."

"What?" She squinted at him from behind her glasses. "That makes no sense."

"About as much sense as you avoiding me the past few weeks."

Maybe she should take pity on him. After all, he had attempted to talk to her a few times in the

NICU when their paths had crossed, but his expression had seemed so forced, his conversation so stilted and underlying with anger that she'd wanted cry. So she'd held fast, avoided him, refusing to become just another woman Ty loved and left by beating him to the punch and keeping distance between them.

"I didn't see you seeking out my company," she pointed out, knowing she probably sounded accusatory.

"Did you want me to seek out your company?"

Had she?

"No."

"Would you have granted me your company if I'd sought you out? Because I got the distinct impression that you wouldn't." He sighed, took her hand in his and studied their locked fingers. "I'm here to find out if you're still going to Texas with me next week."

She'd wondered if he'd want her to, but then had written off the possibility as crazy. Of course he wouldn't want her there. Not after what they'd done. Not after five weeks of awkwardness between them. When she couldn't do more than stutter and blush around him.

"I could see why you might want to reconsider our agreement, but I did keep my end of the deal, which means you owe me."

He really expected her to go with him? Why did that secretly thrill her as much as it scared her? Because she'd missed him and felt desperate for his attention? Lord, she hoped that wasn't it, but feared it just might be.

"Well," she began, glancing toward the computer screen and focusing on a random word, "technically, it was a deal between you and my father, but a deal is a deal, so I really have no choice."

"There's always a choice. If you don't want to go with me, I won't hold you to it."

That got her attention. "Is that your way of telling me you don't really want me to go?"

His expression darkening, he shook his head. "If I didn't want you to go, would I be here talking to you? I want you to go."

What was one weekend with Ty in the grand

scheme of life? She could do this. She'd prove to herself and to him that she could do this and then they'd go back to being just colleagues. Plus, maybe the awkwardness would disappear. "I'll go."

"Hey, Dr. Aston?" With a quick rap on the open door Linda poked her head into the dictation room. "I think you'll want to see this." Noticing Ty sitting next to Eleanor, she added, "That you will both want to see."

Silently, they followed the nurse, pausing just outside the nursery.

"Look who stopped by for a visit," Linda whispered excitedly. "Apparently whatever you said to him when you called made all the difference."

Eleanor's heart quickened at the site of Rochelle's father standing next to his tiny daughter's incubator. It was the first time he'd seen her.

Ty grinned. "I always did think you were one smart woman, Ellie."

Her breath caught at the use of the nickname and she found herself wishing she really did take his breath away each and every time he called her that name. Ellie. How crazy that rather than flinching at the nickname, she wanted to grab the moment and hold it close to her heart?

She cleared her throat. "Babies are smarter than we give them credit for. Rochelle needs her father."

They watched as he gowned, gloved, masked and eyed his baby girl in the incubator. He spoke in a low voice to the little girl. The glistening emotion in his eyes told Eleanor everything he was saying without her being able to hear his actual words.

This was what Rochelle needed. What no tube or medicine or surgical correction could give. She needed her father, the interaction between parent and child.

As if sensing that he was being watched, the man turned, his gaze meeting Eleanor's. "Can I hold her?"

Yes! was all Eleanor could think. Oh, yes! Rochelle needed her father to bond with her, to hold and love her.

Eleanor joined him at the incubator, aware that

Ty stayed just a couple of feet back. She gently went over the proper way for Rochelle's father to hold her, then she prepared the baby to be removed from the isolette.

"If you want to sit in one of the rocking chairs, I'll bring her to you."

Looking uncertain, the man nodded, then did as she'd asked.

"Oh, Rochelle, honey," she told the sweet baby girl. "Today is the day you've been waiting for since you were born. Today you met your daddy and now he's going to hold you and fall hopelessly in love with you."

"You want me to get a bottle to let him try to feed her?" Ty asked from beside her, helping to straighten a wire as Eleanor repositioned the baby.

She glanced at him, smiled. "That would be perfect. She's not been taking much by mouth for the past few days, only by her feeding tube, but maybe, just maybe, today is a day for miracles."

She unhooked what could be unhooked, bundled the babe up and with Ty's assistance they brought the baby to the waiting father.

"You won't go far, will you?" he asked, his eyes full of fear when Eleanor lowered the baby into his arms.

"No, Dr. Donaldson and I will be close. No worries," she assured him, understanding his anxiety as many parents of preemies experienced those same fears. Rochelle's dad probably more so than most as he'd waited weeks to see his daughter. No doubt the man was terrified that his coming here might somehow jinx his baby girl's chances. "If anything changes, we will be right here."

Ty watched the pleased smile spread across Eleanor's face and wondered at the pleasure spreading through him. Of course he was happy that Rochelle's father had finally come to visit his baby girl. But the wonder spreading through him had more to do with the woman he watched.

"Look," Ellie whispered, grabbing his shoulder, her voice breaking with emotion.

Ty's attention returned to Rochelle and her father. The man held the little girl awkwardly, but his eyes were filled with awe, with love.

With unshed tears.

"He's talking to her. I wish I could hear what he's saying," Ellie continued, her voice low, full of just as much emotion as Rochelle's father's.

Ty could almost feel the excitement bubbling through her.

"They're bonding."

Ellie glanced at him, smiled beatifically. "Isn't it wonderful?"

Her smile was wonderful.

Her touch on his shoulder.

The light in her eyes.

He'd missed her.

Something in Ty's chest shifted, blossomed, and he realized that if she'd said no to going to Texas, he'd have talked her into it.

He wanted her with him, wanted to show her his family home, introduce her to his family and, more than anything, he wanted her at his side during the weekend. He'd have begged her to go if that was what it would have taken.

That thought worried him almost as much as the thought of seeing his father again did.

On a plane.

With Tyler Donaldson.

On the way to his family's ranch in Swallow Creek, Texas.

Not feeling a hundred percent as she was fighting a nervous stomach.

How were they going to get through the next few days?

Those were the thoughts running through Eleanor's mind while she pretended to be asleep in the first-class airline seat next to Tyler's.

Pretending to be asleep was easier than trying to make polite conversation as they'd done when their paths had crossed since the day Rochelle's father had come to the NICU. They'd shared a moment of truce when Rochelle's father had been present, but otherwise the awkwardness lingered and made her stomach churn even now.

Then again, everything seemed to make her feel nauseated these days. As a child she'd often had stomach issues when she'd got really nervous or upset, but she'd thought she'd outgrown that during her late teens. Recently, that old habit had returned. As if having to deal with her memories wasn't enough torture.

She snuck a quick peek at the man she couldn't keep from her mind.

And caught him staring at her.

"Good nap?"

"Um, yes. Thanks for asking." Heat infused her face at the way he watched her. As if he knew exactly what she'd been doing.

He couldn't possibly know she'd been faking sleep, could he?

Probably. Somehow Ty seemed to know everything.

The plane hit a bit of turbulence and her stomach lurched. Her face must have paled, because Ty's expression instantly grew concerned. His hand covered hers where she clutched at the armrest.

"You okay?"

For answer, she unbuckled her seat restraint and hurried to the lavatory, grateful that no one was there or she'd have had to make do with the little bag provided on the back of the seat in front of hers.

Once inside the small lavatory, she prayed the other passengers couldn't hear her spilling the meager breakfast she'd forced down.

She prayed Ty couldn't hear.

She delayed in the restroom as long as she dared occupy the only lavatory in first class, but the empathetic gazes that met hers when she left the sanctity of the private space told her everyone had heard.

That Ty had heard.

Great.

Without looking directly at him, she sank into her seat, closed her eyes and said a little prayer that her nerves calmed down. Spending the weekend with Ty was stressful enough. Spending the weekend with him with an upset stomach just went off the charts of bad luck.

"I thought it was me," he mused, "but now I'm wondering if perhaps you just don't enjoy flying."

Her gaze shot toward his. "I'm fine."

"Yes, ma'am," he agreed, his eyes studying her. "I can see that by the ashen color of your skin and the way you're holding your stomach."

Why couldn't she be suave and sophisticated around this man? Why did she continually embarrass herself?

She dug through her purse, searching for a breath mint and popping one into her mouth prior to answering him.

"My stomach acts up sometimes when I get nervous."

"You don't like flying?"

"Th-that's not it."

He considered her answer, then asked, "You're nervous about this weekend? Isn't that my job? You never have to see these folks again. They're my family. I'm stuck with them."

That got her attention, made her stomach lurch. For Ty their relationship was truly temporary. When they returned from Texas, whatever this was between them would well and truly be done. They'd deal with each other at the hospital and nothing more. Which should be just fine by her since she hadn't really expected more of the weekend than fulfilling her end of a deal, had she? She hadn't fantasized that Ty was going to take her into his big Texan arms and tell her he'd missed her as much as she had missed him and that they'd go back to New York as a couple. Nope, no way had she been that gullible and naive.

Willing her stomach to settle because, really, there couldn't be anything left in there, she watched him. "I know you said you and your dad had an argument, but surely you're excited to see your family?"

He didn't look sure.

"How long has it been since you've been home, Ty?" Her question was soft, but had the impact of someone shaking the plane.

"Years." Had Ty made a run for the lavatory and retched, Eleanor wouldn't have been surprised.

She placed her hand over his, meaning to comfort him but only managing to send her pulse into orbit at the flesh-to-flesh contact. Would touching him always affect her so? Always pull her back to memories best forgotten?

They both stared at where her hand covered his, at how her thumb had begun to trace a pattern over his. No, she definitely hadn't had any false hopes where the weekend was concerned.

"You've told me a little about your family, but I'd like to know more before we arrive."

He didn't speak at first and she thought he was going to ignore her or tell her to mind her own business, but finally that sexy Texan drawl of his began to tell her about his life.

"My mother is the greatest woman. Kind, loving, strong. There's nothing the woman can't do. Growing up, I was just as likely to see her out breaking a horse with my father as I was to see her inside, canning vegetables. She wins the bread-baking contest at the county fair every year and has for as long as I can recall. She worked from dawn to late into the night every day, but always found time for my brother and I." He smiled as if a good memory was playing through his mind. "Rarely was there a night that went by that we weren't read a bible story, made to say our prayers, tucked in and kissed good-night by her."

Eleanor smiled at his idealistic-sounding child-hood. How wonderful it must have been to grow up in such a loving family environment. "You said your brother is three years older than you? He's your only sibling?"

He nodded. "Mom wanted more, but there was just us two boys. Probably just as well as we kept her running."

"She sounds wonderful."

"She is." Which meant his mother wasn't anything to do with why he dreaded going home. Then again, he'd already said who it was he didn't get along with.

"Tell me about this father who scares you."

Leaning his head back against the plush first-class seat, Ty snorted. "I was kidding when I said that."

She couldn't imagine him afraid of anything, but there was definitely something off in his relationship with his father.

"Your tone changes when you speak of him," she pointed out in what she hoped was a gentle voice. The skin tightened on his face, too, but she didn't point that out.

He sighed, shifted his hand to where their fingers laced. "I don't talk about my father usually. Life is better that way. Actually, you're the only person I've talked to about him other than my mother and brother."

Why did his admission make her feel as if she was different from the other women he'd been with? That maybe she hadn't imagined just how special their night had been?

"But," he said with another sigh, "since I'm dragging you into the middle of my life, I should prepare you. Can't have you walking in unawares and being blindsided."

"Being blindsided?"

"I told you that the last time I was home my father and I had a disagreement." His lips twisted and a flicker of hurt flashed in his eyes. "I left swearing I'd never set foot in Swallow Creek again."

He still looked at her, but Eleanor wasn't so sure Ty saw her. He looked lost in the past, a dark, unpleasant place that held a tight grip on his present.

She lifted a shoulder. "That's a silly thing to swear about a place where the people you love live."

He blinked, clearing whatever had momentarily come over him. He laughed at her comment, but the sound didn't come out as natural. "You're right, and here I am headed back, ready to eat my words."

Still fighting nausea, she let his admission soak in, trying to understand the man sitting next to her, holding her hand as if she were his lifeline rather than the other way around, as it had been earlier. "Why now? Why go back after all this time? Because of the rodeo?"

He took a deep breath. "My mom's been on me from the moment I left to come back, but she understands my love of medicine." He smiled, thoughts of his mother obviously easing some of his tension. "But lately she's been pushing more and more. With Dad hosting the rodeo this year, she wouldn't let up until I promised I'd be there."

His poor mother must have missed him like crazy and been frantic to repair the rift within her family. But at no point had Ty sounded as if he wanted this trip home.

"Why did you agree if you don't really want to do this?"

He glanced at her, seeming surprised that she'd pushed further. She knew there was more than he was telling her.

"Lots of reasons. I do miss my family." He frowned, then added, "Mostly. Plus, if I don't come home, she and my whole family are going to come to New York for an extended visit."

"Would that be so bad?"

That lopsided grin lifted one side of his handsome face. "Ask me that again after you've met my family."

She smiled, glad to see his usual smile back

in place and hating it that something he'd said nagged at her brain. Hated it because she suspected when she asked him about it his smile was going to slip, but she wanted to understand this man beside her. Which was crazy. After this weekend, they'd probably go back to barely talking to each other.

"You said your mother understood your love of medicine."

There went the smile.

"Does that mean your father doesn't?" she pushed, wondering if her suspicions were correct.

"Let's just say I'm not the son who makes him proud." His jaw working, Ty gave a nonchalant shrug, as if her question was of little consequence, as if his answer was of little consequence. But she saw the clench of his jaw, the quickening pulse at his throat, felt the slight unsteadiness in his hand. His answer revealed a vulnerability in him that made her feel protective, as if she wanted to shield him from anyone who dared to treat him with less than the utmost love and respect.

Which really was crazy.

Ty was a six-foot-four Texan hunk. Not some wallflower who needed her to run interference.

Despite him rescuing her at the ribbon-cutting, the time they'd spent together at the hospital, the fund-raiser and afterward, well, really, they barely knew each other.

Yet she did feel as if she knew him. That he knew her. Really deep down knew each other.

Which was even crazier.

She fought leaning over and taking him into her arms. It was what she wanted to do. She doubted he'd welcome her sympathy, her comfort.

She settled with giving his hand a gentle squeeze and saying quietly, "Then your brother must be an exceptionally amazing man."

CHAPTER EIGHT

THANK GOD HE'D brought Ellie with him, Ty thought for the hundredth time since they'd arrived in Texas. Everyone was so busy falling over themselves to meet the woman he'd brought that no one had mentioned the last time he'd been home.

His mother's welcoming arms squeezed him tightly.

"I'm so glad you're home, son." Her voice broke just a smidge, causing his chest to constrict more than a little. Then she pecked his cheek and turned to the quiet, elegant woman standing at his side. "Eleanor, that's the prettiest skirt I think I've ever laid eyes on. Wherever did you find it?"

First looking at him as if to gauge how he'd responded to his mother's hug and to make sure he was okay, Eleanor turned to his mother and smiled.

"There's this fantastic shop just a couple of blocks from the hospital. It's owned by a family I met when their son was born a couple of weeks early. We've stayed in touch." Her face became animated as she launched into a tale of some of the other bargains she'd found there.

Ty couldn't help but think how pretty she looked. Beautiful, actually. Ellie was beautiful.

He was so glad she was at his side.

From the moment they'd arrived at the airport and been greeted by Harry, Eleanor had been truly wonderful. Despite her bout of travel sickness on the plane, she smiled at all the right times. She asked questions at all the right times. Surprisingly, his shy, quiet Eleanor had even kept up the conversation during the few short, awkward moments that had passed between him and his brother when their father had come up in the conversation.

By the time his brother had helped load their luggage onto the small private twin-engined plane in which Harry would fly them to the ranch, they'd been conversing like, well, like long-lost brothers.

"I'll have to fly up to the city for a shopping trip with you," his mother suggested, still going on about Eleanor's skirt.

Harry and Ty both laughed. Their mother shopping in New York City? She was the most no-nonsense woman they knew, rarely even made it into Houston to shop, and that was only a couple hours' drive away. She rewarded them with a motherly frown.

Ellie glanced back and forth between them, obviously confused by their laughter. She smiled politely at his mother. "That would be nice, but if you do, I'll introduce you to my sister. She's the expert shopper."

Based on the dress she had told him that Brooke had arranged for the ribbon-cutting ceremony, Ty couldn't argue. That dress had accented Eleanor's curves superbly, but the truth was it didn't matter what she wore. Over the past six weeks, seeing her at the hospital in her shapeless scrubs hadn't helped one bit. He knew what she hid beneath and just the memory of her curvy body had his hands itching to touch, had him wanting to beg her to reconsider.

Ty's mother hustled them toward the large eat-in kitchen. When Ty stepped into the room, he breathed in the smell of being home. The room held a lot of memories. Good memories of sitting in here with Harry and his mother while she cooked their breakfast on school mornings. Not-so-good memories of the last row between him and his father, which had also taken place in the room.

Odd, but most of the major conversations of his life had taken place in the Donaldson kitchen.

As if his mother knew exactly what he was thinking about or, more aptly, who, she patted his shoulder. "Your father hated not being able to be here to welcome you home, son, but he had to go to the rodeo to make sure things are coming along on schedule. He's swamped with last-minute details." Her eyes didn't quite meet his, but she pasted another bright smile on her face and hugged him yet again. "Now, let's get the two of you fed. I've left lunch out because I know you must be starved."

Ty's gaze went from his mother to Eleanor. Her thick lashes swept her cheeks. She probably was starved after her bout of travel sickness on the plane. She'd disappeared into the ladies' room at the airport long enough to freshen up and to put her contact lenses in. That had surprised him, but he'd been grateful because nothing blocked his view of her face.

Plus, seeing her without her glasses reminded him of the night of her father's fund-raiser. Which was really a reminder of what had happened after the fund-raiser.

Which made Ty realize he was starved.

But not for food.

Ellie was all he hungered for.

Despite the awkwardness between them since the night they'd spent together, he hadn't stopped wanting her. He missed her and wanted her in his life. And not just at the hospital. Seeing her face light up with a smile did odd things to his insides and he wasn't in denial now.

He wanted her, was going to thoroughly enjoy the next few days of her company, and use the time to convince her they'd shared something special.

"Come along, Ellie. Let's see what my mother has rustled up for us." Ty took her hand in his and grinned at her surprised, pink-cheeked expression at his use of her nickname. Along with the entourage of family who tagged along behind them, he led her to the long solid oak table that matched the cabinets and woodwork.

Harry's son, William, had taken an instant fascination with Eleanor and climbed into the chair opposite hers, staring at her as if she were some big-city goddess. The four-year-old had almost doubled in size since the last time Ty had seen him.

Nita, Harry's wife, chatted a mile a minute about the one time she'd visited New York and how she'd like to come along for his mother's suggested shopping trip, too. His mother busied herself with hostess duties. His brother had kicked back and was watching all the commotion with a lazy grin on his face. Their eyes met and they shared a grin.

Ty's heart squeezed. This was his family. He'd missed them a whole lot more than he'd acknowledged. He should have come home a long time ago, been here for the holidays, been here where William wouldn't have had to rely on the multitude of family photos all over the house to remember who his long-lost uncle Ty was.

But he knew the moment his father got home he'd recall all the reasons he'd left, that within seconds he'd most likely be ready to hop on the first plane back to New York.

"Ellie." His mother used the name she'd heard Ty call her by, concern in her voice. "Is your food not to your liking, dear? I'd be happy to cook something else for you if there's something you'd prefer."

Ty's mind jerked to the present, stunned to realize that he'd demolished every scrap of his mother's delicious home cooking but Eleanor had barely touched her food.

Looking a little pale, she shook her head. "Everything is delicious. I just wasn't that hungry. I'm sorry."

"Don't be sorry, child." His mother's eyes softened as they regarded Eleanor. "If you're not hungry then you're not hungry."

William nudged his mother's arm. "See, Momma, I shouldn't have to clean my plate when I'm not hungry. Grammy says so."

Leaning forward, Harry winked at his son. "You're a growing boy and need your meat and potatoes to make you grow up strong like your old man."

"What he means is like your uncle Ty," Ty corrected, but his eyes never left Eleanor. Her skin had grown pasty, almost a pale gray. "You okay, darlin'? Is your stomach acting up again?"

Bright red color splotched her cheeks as she lifted pleading eyes to him. Eyes that begged to get her somewhere private pronto. Purplish smudges darkened beneath them, almost as if her skin was bruised, and guilt hit him. He'd been so self-absorbed that he'd totally missed that she still wasn't feeling up to par.

"A little," she admitted. "I've never traveled well. Sorry."

His mother must have read her look accurately, too, because before Ty could do more than reach for her hand, she jumped in. "Ty, take this poor girl to your room and let her rest for a bit. She looks exhausted."

His and Ellie's gazes met as realization dawned. He hadn't really thought about where his brother had put her bags. Not in one of the guest rooms as there would be more family coming in for the rodeo and the house would be at full capacity, as would the guesthouse and the bunkhouse. Harry had put her belongings in Ty's room.

Because everyone had assumed she was his girlfriend and that that was where he'd want her sleeping.

That was where he wanted her sleeping. With him.

Of course, if Ellie was in his bed, neither of them would be doing much sleeping.

Then again, with how frail she looked at the moment, he should keep his hands to himself. And other wayward body parts that had a predilection for her.

As much as he wanted her, at the moment he just wanted to take care of her.

"Come on," he said, standing from the table and taking her hand. "Let's get you upstairs for a nap. It's been a long day already since we left LaGuardia this morning."

"I…" she started to argue. He knew that was what she was about to do because her phenomenal etiquette would think it rude to disappear so quickly. But she stopped, which told him just how poorly she felt. Another wave of guilt hit him. How could he have been so lost in his own homecoming misery that he'd been oblivious to her exhaustion and just how much effort she was making to hide how ill she really felt? He felt a grade-A jerk.

He *was* a grade-A jerk.

Because when he'd not been lost in the past, he'd been thinking about the night they'd shared and how he'd been wanting a repetition ever since.

"After our trip this morning, resting for a short while would be heavenly. Thank you." Still, she turned to his mother. "Can I help you clear the dishes before I go?"

His mother beamed at her perfect manners, shot Ty a thumbs-up, I-like-this-girl look. "No, Carmelita has already taken care of everything else so there's only these. She and I will get everything cleaned up in a jiffy. Nita will help."

Watching the conversation curiously, Ty's sister-in-law nodded her agreement.

"You go and rest so you will be refreshed for the rodeo this weekend and meeting the rest of the family. They're all looking forward to meeting the first woman Ty's ever brought home to meet us." As if she couldn't stop herself, his mother pulled her into her arms for a big hug. "We are so glad to meet you, Ellie, and to welcome you to our house and family. This is just wonderful."

* * *

Eleanor bit back both her wince at Ty's mother's use of "Ellie" and the nausea she'd been fighting from the moment she'd smelled food. What was wrong with her? Usually her bouts of nervous stomach didn't last so long.

Then again, usually her bouts of nerves weren't triggered by a trip to Texas with a gorgeous hunk she'd spent a night naked with several weeks ago.

Ha, it had never been triggered by that until Ty and this trip. She'd truly believed he'd have invited someone else or have gone alone.

Not that he'd been linked to anyone since her.

Or if he had, she hadn't gotten the gossip memo.

Since Ty seemed to be Linda's favorite topic of conversation these days, Eleanor was positive she would have heard if Ty had so much as looked in another woman's direction. He hadn't.

Why hadn't he?

He led her up a majestic curved gleaming oak staircase to the second story of the sprawling

Texan mansion that spoke of wealth, function-
ality and family.

Because unlike the magazine picture-perfectness
of her parents' various homes, the Donaldson mansion was filled with love, with family photos and
knickknacks that, without asking, Eleanor knew
had special meaning. The house was lived in and
full of love.

"I like your family," she said when they were
almost to the top of the stairs.

Holding her hand tightly in his, Ty snorted.
"You may want to withhold judgment until you
meet my father. He's the scary one, remember?"

Eleanor's heart squeezed at the pain she heard
in his voice. All her life she'd lived knowing that
she didn't quite fit in with her family, but never
had she doubted that they loved her in their
own way. Even Brooke had her loving-family
moments such as when she'd insisted upon helping Eleanor pack yesterday and had given Eleanor a pair of bright red designer boots for her
trip to Texas. Ty's voice didn't convey that same

knowledge of love. Not where his father was concerned.

"You want to talk about it?"

He shook his head. "No, I just want to get you into bed." He waggled his brows and grinned. "For once not so I can take your clothes off you. Seriously, Ellie, you should have told me you still weren't feeling well. We didn't have to do the whole family thing right then. They can be a bit overwhelming. You could have rested first."

Although she knew he was purposely distracting her from the conversation he didn't want to have, she let him. If he didn't want to tell her about his relationship with his father, what right did she have to pry? After all, she was only the date he had bartered with her father for.

Plus, she really did feel exhausted and so nauseated that she really might throw up again. She hoped not. How embarrassing would that be?

"Honestly, I felt better until we walked into the kitchen. When I smelled the food I just…" She paused, realizing what she'd said and feeling horrible. "I didn't mean that there was anything wrong with your mother's cooking, just that—"

He grinned. "Relax, Ellie. I know what you meant and it's okay." He winked, then opened a door and stepped back for her to enter first.

Immediately on stepping into the room, she was overwhelmed with Ty. With his past and his present. There were all sorts of paraphernalia from his life scattered throughout the darkly masculine room. Obviously at some point his mother had thought the room needed updating to her grown son's tastes, but she hadn't been willing to let go of her little boy either.

"You used to compete in the rodeo?" she asked, walking up to a shelf that was filled with various trophies, plaques and photos of Ty on horses, of Ty roping a calf, of a teenage Ty sliding onto the back of a monstrous-looking cow. "I thought you said you were too tall."

Although he'd paused on stepping into the room, his room, which he hadn't been in for years, that crooked grin of his slid into place. "I'm a true, full-blooded Texan, darlin'. Of course I competed in the rodeo. Besides, I wasn't always this tall."

She gestured to the vast display of awards. "Looks like you were pretty good."

His grin widened and mischief twinkled in his eyes. "Was there ever any doubt?"

She gave him a small smile. "Never. I bet you always won the cow-riding events."

He burst out laughing, slid his hand around her waist and turned her toward the bed. "It's bull riding, darlin'," he corrected her. "Come on. You can check out all this stuff Mom keeps out later. Right now, I want you resting."

He led her to the king-size bed that suddenly dominated the room. They both stopped, stood staring at it.

"You grew up sleeping in this giant bed?" Had her voice just broken?

He shook his head. "Early on Harry and I shared bunk beds. Later, when we went into rooms of our own, I got this furniture. Guess Mom expected us to keep growing."

"She's tiny, so your dad must be a giant of a man."

"He is."

Ty's soft words twisted her heart, made her want to wrap her arms around him and hold him tightly to her.

"You look exhausted, Ellie."

She did feel worn out, which was unlike her. It was probably that she hadn't slept well due to nerves the night before and the travel sickness on the plane had also taken its toll. Yet she couldn't bring herself to climb into Ty's bed so she stood, staring at the big bed.

"Here, let me." He yanked the deep brown comforter back, then gently pushed her down onto the bed in a sitting position.

What he did next surprised her. More like stunned her.

He dropped to his knees, slipped her shoes off her feet and set them aside. His hands slid up her calves, massaged along the way, paused at her knees, leaning forward and kissing each one, then, over her skirt, up her thighs, her hips, to her waist.

He placed his palms against her upper arms and gently guided her backward. "Lie back, Ellie, and take a load off."

She did, letting him pull the covers around her and tuck her in as if she were a small child, then he straightened, stood staring at her with an odd look in his eyes.

Suddenly she felt terribly alone in the big bed. "Ty, hold me."

His brows went together in a surprised V, but he kicked off his shoes and slid into the bed next to her.

He wrapped his arms around her, held her close to him in spoon fashion and dropped a kiss on her hair. "Now, close your eyes and be very still, Ellie, or else we're going to have a problem."

It only took her a second to realize what he meant. Giddiness bubbled up inside her. She twisted around to face him, stared into his beautiful eyes and couldn't keep from smiling.

"You really find me attractive, don't you?"

He gave her a quizzical look. "Why wouldn't I find you attractive? You are a beautiful, amazing, sexy woman, Ellie. Any man would have to be blind not to find you attractive." He slid his palm over the curve of her hip. "Of course a blind man would have to feel his way. Then he'd know how hot you were firsthand, too."

Eleanor's insides melted. Unable to stop herself, she stretched forward and closed the distance between their lips. Just a soft brushing of her lips against his. It was the first time they'd kissed since the night of the fund-raiser. Instantly, longing shot through her. Longing for the way she'd felt that night. Longing for the way she felt at this very moment, touching him.

"Now you're just tempting fate," he warned in a low voice. "You're supposed to be resting."

She blinked at him, not so innocently. "What if I don't feel so very tired anymore?"

Amazingly, she didn't. That was crazy, as moments before just holding her head up had almost required too much effort, but lying in Ty's arms, kissing him, energized her, cured her fin-icky stomach.

His brow arched, a boyish grin on his face, his eyes twinkling with delight. "Darlin', were you playing possum to get me into bed and take advantage of me?"

Her gaze not wavering from his, she shook her head and with great clarity knew exactly what she wanted. "No, but kiss me, Ty. Kiss me as if you mean it."

His expression growing serious, his eyes darkened. "I do mean it, Ellie. When I kiss you, I mean every touch."

She wasn't sure what he meant by his words or even what she'd meant by her request. Not until his lips touched hers.

Then she knew.

He kissed her softly and slowly, yet with an undercurrent of urgency that let her know he wanted more, that he struggled to keep from deepening the kiss. His hands ran over her body just as softly and slowly, as if she were a prize to be treasured.

That was how he made her feel, how he'd made her feel that night. Like she was the most important woman in the whole world to him. Like she was the only woman.

For now that was enough.

That was everything.

CHAPTER NINE

ELEANOR'S NOSE WRINKLED even before they stepped inside the long sheet-metal building they were headed toward, which Ty called the main barn. There was a definite outdoorsy smell to the cold, crisp February Texas air. Fortunately, her nausea had completely passed.

As had her fatigue.

Amazing what phenomenal sex did for a person.

And the sex *had* been phenomenal. Part of her had wondered if her recall of how fantastic Ty was had been due to too many glasses of the champagne she'd consumed.

Definitely not.

They'd napped for an hour or so afterward. Now she just felt great.

She snuggled more fully into the thick coat Ty's mother had insisted she wear when they'd headed out the door and she'd only had her over-coat. His mother had also found her a pair of boots to put on so she didn't have to worry about soiling her shoes.

"I like your family, Ty." Not that she'd met his father yet. The great man had yet to return from the arena where the rodeo was being held. Her breath made a puff of smoke in the crisp air.

"Good." He clasped her gloved hand. "They like you, too."

Her gaze cut toward him as they continued their trek toward the barn. "Am I really the first girl you've brought home?"

Staring at her from beneath the cowboy hat he'd donned before they'd left his bedroom, he feigned a sigh. "Caught that, did you?"

"What can I say?" She smiled, despite the frigid air stinging her face. "Smart chick, re-member?"

He turned to look at her, his eyes like molten chocolate. "I remember everything about you, Ellie."

At the warmth in his voice, her insides lit.

"But to answer your question, there were a few local girls during high school who came to the ranch. But during college and afterward…" he shrugged beneath the heavy work coat he'd donned "…I just didn't meet anyone I wanted to bring to Swallow Creek."

"You brought me." Her heart slammed against her rib cage. She knew it didn't mean anything, that she'd only been a convenient, uncomplicated buffer between his family and the circumstances under which he'd left Swallow Creek.

Only more and more her relationship with Ty wasn't feeling convenient or uncomplicated.

Sex complicated everything.

"A wise decision on my part."

Uncertainty hit her. "Because of what happened in your room?"

He pushed an aluminum door open, pulled her inside the building. Warmth swamped her as she stepped onto the concrete floor. Her idea of a "barn" was nothing like the extensive heated metal building in which they stood. This was more like a minibusiness complex. She supposed it was. At the far end she could see areas that appeared to be stables, but at this end there were office spaces and everything was quite meticulous.

Ty shed his gloves, unzipped his jacket and pulled it off. "What just happened was fantastic, but that wasn't what I meant. I meant because I enjoy being with you—your company, your smile, just holding your hand."

"Oh."

Grinning, he rubbed his finger across her cold nose. "Yeah…oh."

After taking her coat, gloves and scarf and hanging them, along with his, in one of the small offices, he took her hand and showed her around the main barn, one of several barns on the Triple D, apparently. He introduced her to some of the hands, let her feed an apple to a mare, then proudly showed her his stallion, Black Magic.

"Why have a horse when you've not been home for years, Ty?"

He stared at the horse, his expression contemplative. "He's a Thoroughbred and a champion, so he brings a high stud fee." He'd shown her a room earlier where those stud fee samples were kept frozen. "That more than pays for his upkeep, but maybe you're right. Maybe I should sell him as I'm not around."

Eleanor glanced back at the magnificent animal that snorted and grunted as if giving his own feedback to his long-gone owner. Something in Ty's tone said he didn't want to let the horse go, that really he was ready to heal past wounds, but perhaps Ty himself wasn't even aware of what she heard.

"Or maybe," she suggested softly, hoping she wasn't overstepping the boundaries of their tentative, confusing relationship, "you should come home and ride him more often."

Ty held Ellie's hand tightly in his as they walked into the Swallow Creek Arena where the rodeo was being held. Tonight's agenda was more about family fun and kicking off the rodeo than actual competitions. There were kids' events, exhibits, a barbecue cook-off and a barn dance.

From the time they made their entrance, familiar faces greeted Ty, introduced themselves to Eleanor and told him how good it was to see him.

No one mentioned his father.

But no doubt about it, he'd be seeing his father soon.

Acid gurgled in his stomach.

He glanced at Ellie in her jeans and Western-style snap-up that his sister-in-law had insisted she wear. It seemed his whole family was planning to dress her before the weekend ended, but Ellie took it all in her stride, smiling and going along with their wardrobe suggestions.

The jeans were a little snug and looked good clinging to her body. The shirt did nothing to hide her generous curves and looked even better. Ty's mouth watered just recalling what those curves felt like in his hands, his mouth, pressed to his body.

And the boots. There wasn't a single practical thing about Ellie's red boots but hell if they weren't his favorite part about her outfit. Somehow the bright boots suited her, the real her, the passionate woman beneath the surface.

"You okay?" she asked, her big eyes looking up at him.

"Fine," he answered, squeezing her hand gently. "I'm fine, darlin'. Just so long as I have you at my side."

Which crazily enough was true. Having her next to him both excited and calmed him.

"Just thinkin' how much I liked your boots." He grinned, liking how her gaze dropped to her boots and a blush that almost matched their bright color spread across her cheeks. "And what's in 'em," he added, just to watch the color in her cheeks deepen.

"Ty Donaldson?" a familiar feminine voice called out from behind them with a distinctive Southern drawl. "Is that really you?"

"Layla?" Ty spun, surprise filling him at the sight of the pretty little blonde barreling toward him. He held his arms out and she stepped into them. "Layla! What are you doing here? Last I heard you were practicing in Florida."

She hugged him then smiled up at him as if he was a sight for sore eyes. "I'm still in Miami. How about you? You still a big-city doc up North?"

"Absolutely. Angel's is where I was meant to be. There's no place in the world I'd rather practice than at that hospital."

Ellie shifted at his side and he put his arm at her waist, proudly pulling her close to him. "Excuse my been-away-from-the-South-too-long rudeness, Layla. This is Dr. Eleanor Aston. She's a pediatrician at Angel's. One of the best. Y'all have a lot in common."

Eleanor told herself that it didn't mean a thing that Ty introduced her as a coworker and not as his weekend date. Or that he'd introduced her as "Eleanor" rather than the "Ellie" he'd taken to calling her by. Or that when he'd said they had a lot in common she'd instantly wondered if he meant they'd both slept with him.

She was just being overly sensitive when there was no reason. But when the petite woman had launched herself into Ty's arms, Eleanor had felt overly sensitive, gawky and jealous.

Jealous. Her. She really wasn't the jealous type.

She winced. She had no claims to Ty. None whatsoever. Yet…

She was jealous of the slender young woman Ty grinned at as if she were his long-lost best friend.

"Layla is the daughter of Swallow Creek's longtime mayor, Rick Woods. She was one of my closest friends from school."

Okay, so maybe she was his long-lost best friend. Or did he mean closest as in former girlfriend? Hating the way she was reacting, Eleanor pulled in her little green monster and accepted the smiling woman's outstretched hand.

"I have Ty to thank for encouraging me to go into medicine," Layla said, shaking Eleanor's hand with enthusiasm. "I owe him big-time."

"Hmm." Ty scratched his chin. "Then maybe you should consider moving up North so you can pay your debt."

Eleanor's gaze jerked to him, but she couldn't

read anything beyond the friendly grin on his relaxed face. Was he flirting with the woman? What was she thinking? Of course Ty was flirting. It was what he did with every woman.

Layla gave him a confused look. "What would I do up North?"

"More good than you'd believe possible. You should come and work at Angel's."

Layla gave him a thoughtful look. "Why do you say that?"

"Although nothing's official, the current head of Pediatrics is going to make a career change. Soon. You'd be the perfect person to take his place."

Interest flickered on the blonde's face, but she still looked hesitant.

"You'd like working at Angel's, Layla. Those kids reach in, grab your heart and don't let go. The entire hospital is about serving others, giving to those in need. If ever I question my life choices, all I have to do is step into that hospital to know I'm exactly where I'm meant to be, helping those who can't help themselves."

Eleanor bit her lower lip. Ty was right, of course. There was no place like Angel's. While she stood, feeling more and more out of place, they chatted about Angel's awhile longer, about Ty's family, about a couple of mutual friends.

"Have you seen Luke since you've been home?"

Her smile fading and her expression growing guarded at Ty's question, Layla shook her head. "I'm just here for a few days to visit with Mom and Dad."

"That going okay?"

A smile that Eleanor could only describe as sad slid onto the woman's face. "Probably about as well as your visit. How's your father?"

"Right." Ty laughed, put his arm around Eleanor's waist, instantly making her feel a little better. What was wrong with her? She shouldn't be jealous of his easy camaraderie with the woman. It wasn't as if she hadn't seen him talk to hundreds of women at Angel's. Then again, perhaps she'd never really liked that either.

His thumb rubbing across the indent at

Eleanor's lower back, toying with the waistband of her jeans, Ty's gaze remained on Layla. "Why don't you come grab a seat with Ellie and me? We'll tell you more about the Angel Mendez Children's Hospital and why you should think about joining our team."

Ellie. He'd called her Ellie. Instantly, the tension that had been gripping her shoulders eased and she let out the breath she hadn't even realized she'd been holding. Who would have ever thought that the nickname would make her feel better instead of worse?

"You're sure I wouldn't be intruding?" Layla looked back and forth between Ty and Eleanor.

Reining in the remainder of her green monster, Eleanor shook her head. "No, please do. I want to hear all about Ty's youth. Maybe you could tell me some good stories for me to tease him about."

Layla smiled back, hooked her arm through Eleanor's and began to do just that.

Later, Eleanor admitted that she liked the beautiful young doctor from Ty's past. It hadn't hurt that he'd kept Eleanor close, holding her hand while they talked, asking for her input regarding Angel's. That Layla had been sweet, friendly and not once had she looked at Ty in any way that made Eleanor feel uncomfortable. Once she'd gotten over her initial jealousy, she'd realized that nothing more than friendship had ever existed between the two.

The three of them had eaten barbecue and laughed at some of the children's antics during the kids' events. They'd laughed at some of the animals' antics, too.

With a heartfelt sigh Layla excused herself when her mother motioned to her. Eleanor and Ty continued to check out exhibits, talk to his old friends and generally enjoy the chaos that was apparently the rodeo. They remained all smiles until a giant of a man stepped up beside them and slapped Ty on the back

Without really looking at the man's features, Eleanor knew who he was.

Ty's body language did a one-eighty from relaxed and happy to tight and agitated. All without the man saying a single word.

Just a touch and his father sent him into an obvious tailspin.

"You ready to pack up and come home from that big city to be a real man?"

Had his father's first words to Ty in years really been those? Next to her, Ty's spine straightened and she felt the tension bristling within him.

She wasn't exactly sure what she should do, but she knew she needed to do something to defuse the situation before sparks flew. She stuck out her hand and politely introduced herself. "Hi, I'm Eleanor Aston. You must be Ty's father."

The older man turned astute golden-brown eyes toward her. Definitely, she'd have recognized him as Harry and Ty's father. The likeness was strong with the man's handsome but more weathered face and tall- body build. But that was where the similarities ended because, whereas Ty was always smiling and oozing charm, this man's face bore a scowl that appeared permanently etched into his features.

"You are?" he asked.

Ty's jaw clenched and she could feel him counting forward, backward, asking for patience to keep from reacting to his father.

"Ty's big-city guest from New York. Born and raised and absolutely love it there." Had that confident, almost sassy reply really been her? Without a single stutter? Wow. Generally, she was all about keeping the peace but this man obviously had no real appreciation for the wonderful son he had. Any man who was too blind to see Ty for his true self didn't register too highly in her opinion.

His father's expression remained unreadable, but before he could respond Ty spoke. "Great to see you, too, Dad. Layla's home for the rodeo, too."

Ignoring the first part of Ty's comment, his father shook his head as if in disgust. "A shame that you two were raised right and both took off for parts unknown to take care of babies. Her I can understand. She's a woman." His expression slipped into one of true confusion. "But you? My son? Babies?"

Apparently Ty's dad lived in another century. Eleanor slipped her hand into Ty's and gave it a reassuring squeeze. "That's what neonatologists do. There's no nobler profession than to save lives and who better to save than precious newborn babies?"

"Ellie—" Ty began, but didn't finish as they were interrupted.

"There you two are!" His mother stepped up, all smiles, but her gaze went back and forth anxiously between Ty and his father. "Harold, Harry was looking for you. William is up in a few. He thought you might have a few words of advice prior to his turn. You're so good at that kind of thing."

The giant of a man Ty called his father looked at his wife as if he knew exactly what she was doing, but he just nodded. "Fine, I'll go talk to the boy." His gaze went back to Ty, dropped to where his and Eleanor's hands were clasped, then he shook his head. "Ain't like there's a lot to riding a sheep, though, and he didn't need my input when he won the calf-roping competition. That boy may only be four, but he has been taught right."

His father mumbled a few more things that Eleanor didn't quite catch before he disappeared through the crowd to go and encourage his grandson. At least, she hoped he was going to encourage his grandson. After how he'd interacted with Ty she had to wonder if the man knew how.

His mother gave them an apologetic look, then took off after her husband, no doubt to grill him about what he'd been saying to Ty. Good. Eleanor hoped she gave him an earful.

"Wow," she breathed, glancing up at Ty. "You weren't kidding when you said he didn't approve of your medical career."

"Nope."

Ty's expression remained tight, withdrawn. She didn't like it, wanted back the closeness they'd shared all evening, all day really. But she didn't know what to say because she didn't understand Ty's father's reaction to his son. How could any man not be proud of a son like Ty, who dedicated his life to helping those in need?

Since words failed her, she lifted his hand to her lips and pressed a soft kiss there. "You are a wonderful doctor, Tyler Donaldson. Your patients and their families think you are wonderful. You have a special gift and everyone at Angel's benefits from you being there. Me included." She paused, took a deep breath. "Actually, me especially."

His gaze met hers, darkened. "Thank you, Ellie. I needed that." His hand slipped around her waist, pulling her in for a hug. He bent, whispered in her ear, "I needed you."

Ty held Ellie tightly in his arms, his face close to her hair, breathing in her lightly seductive scent while they danced on the crowded dance floor.

All evening he'd found himself touching her. Her hand. Her face. Her arms. Her back. Anywhere just to reassure himself that she was really there, that she was real.

All evening he'd found his gaze meeting hers, knowing what she was thinking, sharing secret smiles, laughing at her comments over some of the events, proud to show her off to his childhood friends and family, anxious to get her home so he could peel off her jeans and have her and those red boots all to himself.

"I know I'm not the best at Texas two-stepping." Her startled voice broke into his thoughts. "But did you just growl at me?"

Ty grinned at the woman in his arms. Tonight could have been horrible, a blast from the past, but, thanks to her, it hadn't. With the exception of when he'd come face-to-face with his father, he'd actually had a great time. "Maybe. Did I?"

"I believe you did."

"I guess you bring out the growl in me."

Her arms around his neck, her face bright with happiness, she laughed. "Thank you, Ty."

He couldn't help but want to lock the magical sound away inside him to pull out on some rainy day. Ellie's laughter could chase away clouds, could chase away Texas tornadoes.

"I've had fun tonight," she continued, missing a step and landing on his toes. "Oops!" She gave him a little apologetic look, then smiled and added, "More fun than I can remember having in a long time."

"Me, too, Ellie." He slid his fingers beneath her chin, lifted her face, stared into her lovely brown eyes. "But for the record the night isn't over and what comes later is a lot more fun."

Her gaze locked with his, she nodded her understanding, smiled. "Promises, promises."

"No worries, darlin'." He dropped a kiss on the tip of her nose. "I'm a man of my word."

"You really were good at riding, weren't you?" Eleanor asked later that night while lying in the crook of Ty's arms in his big king-size bed.

His bare chest rumbling with amusement, he tickled her side. "You should already know the answer to that firsthand."

Feeling almost decadent, she giggled and

squirmed against him. "I am not a horse or a cow, Tyler Donaldson."

Within seconds he had her pinned beneath him and grinned. "No, but you ride like a—"

Laughing, her mouth dropped open and she feigned looking aghast, and his head lowered, brushed a kiss across her parted lips.

He waggled his brows. "Sorry, couldn't resist."

"Try harder next time."

"I'll give you hard." Proof of his claim pressed against her hip.

"Ty!"

"Now, say it again," he teased, his eyes telling her exactly what he meant, what he intended. "This time with more feeling."

He kissed her. Over and over.

When his name next left her lips he didn't have to ask for more feeling, for more of anything.

She gave him everything she had within her to give.

CHAPTER TEN

THE NEXT MORNING Ty woke with a jerk as Ellie shot out of bed and rushed to the bathroom. Startled out of a deep peaceful sleep, his bare feet had barely hit the cold hardwood floor when the sound of her retching met his ears.

Was she okay? Too much barbecue and sex the night before? Or had her travel sickness not ever completely cleared?

Without a word he entered the bathroom, got a cold, wet washcloth and placed it to her clammy forehead.

Looking miserable, she knelt next to the toilet, her shoulders slumped, her body quivering, her eyes closed.

"I'd ask if you're okay, but obviously you're not." He hated the thought of her not feeling well. He was a doctor, should be able to do something to ease her symptoms. "You want a drink of water?"

She nodded ever so slightly as if she was afraid that any movement might trigger another round of losing any remaining contents of her stomach.

He took a disposable paper cup from a dispenser on the sink and filled it with cool water. She took the cup, swished the water around her mouth and spat in the toilet several times.

"I'm so embarrassed," she said in a weak voice, her eyes squeezed tightly shut. "I hate that you saw me like this."

"Now I know why you don't stick around for mornings-after," he teased in reference to the morning she'd tried to leave before he'd awakened.

To the morning several weeks ago.

The morning after… Oh, hell.

The floor shifted beneath Ty's feet and his toes gripped the cold tile in the hope of maintaining his balance.

"That's not why I was leaving that morning," Ellie moaned, sounding miserable, oblivious to the crazy thoughts rushing through his head. "I just didn't know what we'd say to each other or how you'd feel. Or—"

"Ellie," he interrupted, his hand against the wall to balance himself. Sweat popped up on his brow, on the back of his neck. "Are you sure you just have a nervous stomach?"

Please say yes.

Misery on her pale face, she shrugged. "I've had a nervous stomach on and off most of my life. It just hadn't bothered me in years until…"

His heart slammed against his rib cage in thunderous bursts. His mind raced ahead, drawing what he hoped were inaccurate conclusions. "Not until the past couple of weeks?"

Face pink, she nodded again. "Yes. I was anxious about coming here with you, Ty. I'm really sorry I woke you up to this. I kept lying there thinking my nausea would pass, but it just kept getting worse. I couldn't hold it back any longer."

His heart beating faster and faster, his insides shaking, his knees threatening to buckle, he sank down to the floor next to her, placed his hand on her thigh. "Ellie, have you had a menstrual cycle since the night we first made love?"

Her lips didn't move, but they didn't have to. The widening of her eyes and blanching of her skin answered for her.

She hadn't.

Dear Lord, Ellie might be pregnant with his baby.

Eleanor shook. Her entire body *shook.*

Pregnant.

Was that even a possibility?

Well, of course it was a possibility. She and Ty had had sex. About a month ago.

She had missed her menstrual cycle.

She'd been so lost in thoughts about the night she'd spent with Ty, about this upcoming trip, that she'd never even noticed that she'd skipped a period. Could she be any more naive?

"I'm probably only late due to stress." Surely that was the only reason she hadn't gotten her period.

"Are you usually regular?" He sounded so

calm, so logical. If not for the tremble of his hand where he touched her thigh, she might think him completely unaffected.

She closed her eyes and nodded. "Yes. Usually I'm like clockwork."

"Have your breasts been more sensitive?"

She so did not want to be having this conversation. Not while crouched on the bathroom floor. Naked. With Ty. Naked. With her having just thrown up.

Under the best of circumstances she didn't want to be having this conversation, but definitely she didn't under the current ones.

A new wave of mortification hit her and she wrapped her arms around her body, trying to cover herself, wishing she could just crawl back into the fantastic dream she'd been having prior to waking and making her mad dash to the bathroom.

"Ellie," Ty whispered, wrapping his arms fully around her and holding her tightly to him. "Oh, Ellie, you're pregnant, aren't you?"

"I…I don't know. It—it never occurred to

me that I might be." She kept her eyes tightly squeezed shut, hating that hot tears stung her eyelids, hating that she'd stuttered. "It's possible." She sucked in a breath, praying she didn't hiccup or sob. "I'm sorry, Ty."

She felt his fingers clasp her chin, felt him lifting her face, but she didn't open her eyes, couldn't bear to see what was in his eyes.

"Look at me."

She prised her eyelids apart, not surprised that the moment she did so the waterworks started down her cheeks.

"Don't cry, darlin'." He wiped at her tears. His hands were soft, gentle, attempting to comfort, but just the thought of what might be had her insides crumbling.

"If you are pregnant, you didn't get that way alone," he continued. "I'm as much to blame as anyone. More so."

To blame. Because this wasn't something good. Wasn't something planned for. She might be having a baby and rather than it being a joyous discovery, she sat naked on a bathroom floor, being coddled by a man who couldn't possibly want to be here but was. He was being sweet and wonderful rather than angry.

Which made her feel all the more guilty that she hadn't been suave and sophisticated like the women he was used to, like no doubt her own sister was.

"We weren't exactly thinking straight that night," she whispered, offering him an out.

"All I was thinking that night was that I wanted you, Ellie, but that doesn't excuse me making love to you without a condom. All I can say is that I've never done that before. I've never wanted someone so much that I lost control that way."

She bet he didn't want her now. Not after seeing her like this. She probably repulsed him.

But rather than pull away, he just held her to him for long moments, kissing the top of her head and gently rocking her in his arms while she cried.

Which probably only added to how bad she looked.

When he stood, he got another damp wash-cloth, knelt and gently cleaned away her tears. "You feel like standing up?"

She took a deep breath and nodded, although really she wasn't sure of anything. Her legs felt weak and her head spun, but they couldn't stay like this forever.

He took her hand and helped her to her feet. "Let's get a shower, get dressed, then we'll go into town and buy a pregnancy test. No use worrying about this until we know exactly what we're worrying about. Maybe it really is just your nerves."

He didn't sound hopeful, but perhaps…

Really, if it was just her nerves, that would be best all the way around. Yet the idea that Ty's baby might be growing inside her… She placed her hand on her belly. Was there a baby there? Her and Ty's baby?

Why did she hope not?

But, even more confusing, why did the thought not seem so horrible either?

When he'd suggested taking a shower, she'd

thought he'd meant alone. Honestly, she wanted to be alone, to have a few minutes to herself to think, digest the morning's events. But he must have been afraid to leave her, because he turned the walk-in shower on, tested the temperature then pulled her in with him.

He didn't say a word, just washed her hair, her body, rinsed her clean, then did the same for himself while she watched.

When he was done, he wrapped her in a large bath sheet and they silently dressed.

She wished she knew what he was thinking. Considering what might be happening inside her body, he'd been wonderful, sweet, very understanding.

But he couldn't be happy about the possibility of her being pregnant with his child. Of all the women he'd ever been with, he'd surely have chosen someone different to have conceived his child.

What about her? How did she feel about all the things bouncing around in her head?

What if before the end of the year she was going to give birth to Ty Donaldson's baby?

"You've barely said two words since we left the house," Ty pointed out as he maneuvered Ole Bess into downtown Swallow Creek.

Ellie sat with her hands folded in her lap, staring out the passenger window at the various businesses they drove past. "At this point, I'm not sure what to say."

She'd been quiet all morning. Somehow she'd made it through breakfast with his family, although she'd barely eaten a thing until his mother had yet again offered to have something different prepared. Red-faced, Ellie had forced down some eggs and a biscuit, but he'd seen the effort she'd put into doing so, had held her hair away from her face as she'd paid for those efforts in the lavatory not twenty minutes later.

Had he done that to her?

"If you are pregnant, we'll figure something out, Ellie." Guilt rode him hard. "You have to know I won't leave you to deal with this on your own."

"I won't have an abortion." For the first time that day her voice had strength and she met him square in the eyes. "I won't do that."

"I wouldn't ask you to." Ty winced. Had she thought he would when they worked day and night to save babies?

"I'm sorry." She turned away from him, stared out the window, her hands clenching and un-clenching in her lap. "I didn't mean to imply that you would. I was just stating a fact."

"I understand."

He did. If she was pregnant, her entire life would change. His, too, but Ellie's in a more im-mediate way as her body grew with their baby.

Their baby. In his mind, she was already preg-nant.

Ellie was pregnant.

In his heart, he knew she was. He'd been around animals his entire life, had dealt with nature on the ranch. He should have recognized the possibility of her being pregnant when they'd been on the plane and she'd been sick.

Then again, she'd written off her illness as a nervous stomach so perhaps he could be forgiven.

"Do you even want kids, Ty?"

Her voice was tiny, vulnerable, so full of need that he pulled into the parking lot of a general mart and killed the truck engine, rather than driving to the other side of town to the chain pharmacy where they might have a little anonymity. They probably wouldn't have, but it had been a thought.

He undid his seat belt and turned to her. "I can't say that I've given much thought to the idea of having kids, Ellie. Maybe I thought I would someday, but up to this point in my life, taking care of the babies at Angel's has been enough."

She nodded as if she understood. Perhaps she did. Perhaps she felt the same.

"But if you are pregnant with my child, I will

want our baby and I will do right by you and our child. Don't doubt that."

"With your…" Her startled gaze met his, wide-eyed and full of shock. "There's no possibility of my being pregnant by anyone other than you."

"Not what I meant." He raked his fingers through his hair, wondering if he was destined to repeatedly say the wrong thing today. "Let's go buy the test. See if there's a reason for us to discuss this further and we'll go from there, okay?"

Her cheeks pink, she nodded.

Of all the stores in Swallow Creek, he would have to choose the one where Nita just happened to be.

"Ty? Ellie?" she exclaimed when she spotted them in the checkout line. "I didn't know y'all were headed to town."

Ty considered putting the box behind his back, but figured that would only draw Nita's attention to what he held. Not that he needed to worry. She noticed anyway.

Her eyes growing huge, Nita's jaw dropped, her hands clasped together.

"Are you pregnant?" she gasped, much louder than Ty would have liked. Surely everyone in the general mart was now staring, waiting for Ellie to answer.

Ellie's cheeks glowed a bright pink and she didn't seem capable of answering. Perhaps she wasn't.

"Mind your own business, Nita. Besides, if we knew the answer to that question, we wouldn't have need for this, now, would we?" He motioned to the rectangular box he held.

Looking way too excited, Nita said, "Your mother said Ellie was pregnant, but I didn't—"

"Mom said what?" he gasped. If Ellie was pregnant, they needed time to digest the news, time to figure out what they wanted, time without his family butting in. His mother knew?

A sinking feeling gripped his gut. If his mother knew, his father would soon know.

Nita smiled, knowing she'd snagged his attention. "Yesterday, after the two of you went upstairs after lunch, she said that Ellie was pregnant, but the rest of us thought she was just doing some wishful thinking out loud."

His entire family had been debating the possibility of Ellie being pregnant before either of them had suspected a thing?

"Wishful thinking?" he muttered, still trying to wrap his mind around how his mother was so observant she'd figured out quickly what he'd missed. He was a doctor. Then again, she'd lived on a farm or ranch her entire life and was on a first-name basis with Mother Nature. He was pretty sure they sat down for tea on a regular basis.

"You know how she wants more grandkids to spoil rotten," Nita reminded him, beaming at Ellie.

"So you and Harry give her a few more."

"Ty?" Ellie's voice sounded panicky. She reached out, clutched his upper arm as if for support.

His gaze immediately went to her pale face.

"I think I'm going to pass out."

Then she did.

He caught her just before she hit the floor.

Two blue lines. Pregnant.

Eleanor was grateful she was sitting on the shiny oak floor of Ty's bathroom, that she was leaning up against the wall, that Ty sat beside her, holding the test so they could look at the results together.

His hand shook as he held it out for them both to read.

She closed her eyes, took a deep breath and looked at the results again.

There were still two blue lines.

Positive.

Eleanor Aston, the other Aston daughter, the quiet, shy Aston, pregnant out of wedlock.

The media would have a field day.

Her father would have a fit.

Recalling how he'd arranged her date with Ty, perhaps he wouldn't have a fit. Perhaps he'd find an angle, hand out cigars and ask for votes in his upcoming election. Or he'd take out his proverbial shotgun and demand Ty make an honest woman of her, probably just so he could marry her off to a well-to-do Texan while he had an excuse to push the issue.

Her mother would be mortified and remind her not to eat too much because losing baby fat wasn't going to be an easy feat.

Brooke would… What would her sister say? Probably high-five her on getting "knocked up by such a scrumptious man." But that was Brooke. Always thinking in the short term, never the long term.

Then again, maybe she was more like her sister than she'd thought. Because she certainly hadn't been thinking the long term on the night she'd gone to Ty's apartment.

Everything had been about short-term pleasure.

Now there were long-term consequences.

She was having his baby.

"I'm sorry," she whispered, for lack of knowing what else to say as she stared at the test he held in trembling fingers.

"Quit saying that you're sorry, Ellie." He almost sounded angry that she'd done so again. "I don't want you to be sorry."

She winced. Poor Ty. She'd gone out like a light in the general mart and he'd carried her back to the truck while Nita had paid for the pregnancy test. How many times had she apologized for that one? At least a few dozen on the ride back to the ranch. No doubt his entire family knew what had happened by now. Probably the entire town knew. Ty's hometown, and she'd embarrassed him. She was pregnant with his baby. Her face flamed.

"But it's true." She wished she could convey to him how humiliated she felt that she'd passed out, how sorry she was that she wasn't sophisticated enough to have prevented pregnancy. After all, she knew better, but on the night they'd made love she just hadn't been thinking. She'd like to blame the champagne, but she wasn't sure how much had been alcohol and how much had been pure Ty. "I didn't mean to get pregnant."

He set the test down on the floor beside him.

"I know that, but we're talking about a human life that we've created." His expression gentled. "Don't be sorry for a new life. Don't ever be sorry for that."

"But it wasn't intentional." She needed to be sure he understood that.

"Most babies aren't intentionally created. You know that. That doesn't make those babies any less special, any less lovable. We made a baby, Ellie. A new life isn't a bad thing."

She stared at him, wondering if she was dreaming. If, when she'd passed out, she'd hit her head and was now living in some fantasy world. "You're taking this too well."

He leaned his head back against his bathroom wall, took a deep breath and gave a slight shrug. "Honestly, I'm not sure how I'm taking anything, Ellie. I'm blown away."

That she understood.

"We're having a baby."

Not that she was having a baby, but "we're." He'd said "we're."

She closed her eyes. "What are you going to tell your family?"

Head down, he snorted. "Nita will already have told Harry and my mother that she saw us at the store. Plus, my mother already knew. Hell, you heard Nita. The entire family was debating if you were or not."

She dropped her head forward, resting her forehead against her knees.

"I didn't know." How could she have been so oblivious? Then again, why should she have suspected? Pregnancy wasn't something she'd given any thought to. "I honestly hadn't considered the possibility of being pregnant until you asked about my cycle. I feel stupid that I hadn't, but I just never…well, you know."

He laced his fingers with hers, held her hand tightly within his, rubbing his thumb gently over her skin. "I know. Shock was written all over your face."

"Better you were looking at my face than the rest of me this morning," she mumbled, recalling how horrid she must have looked on the bathroom floor.

Odd that they were back there now. At least

now they were fully dressed and she hadn't just thrown up the contents of her stomach.

Although certainly the news that she was pregnant was enough to have her stomach pitching and rolling.

Ty squeezed her hand. "I happen to like looking at the rest of you, darlin'. I like it a lot. Perhaps you noticed. I did a lot of looking yesterday afternoon and during the night."

He sounded so sure, so sincere, yet he couldn't be, could he? Yet he had acted as if he enjoyed her body. Maybe he was just one of those men who loved women, period, and it didn't matter how curvy they were.

"I'm going to gain a lot of weight." Just the mental image of what she'd look like in a few months made her want to cringe. "I won't be one of those cute pregnant women who maintain their body with a basketball for a belly. I'll just look like the basketball. A big, giant basketball."

His gaze narrowed and he forced her to look at him. "Your body is going to change into the body of a pregnant woman who is carrying my child. Mine. There's nothing more beautiful, Ellie."

Her insides quivered, and she found herself wanting to lean on him, put her head on his shoulder and put her trust in him. "I want to believe you, but…"

"But?"

"I know I'm not exactly the stuff of legends right now. How are you going to want me when I'm larger?" The tears had started flowing. Lots and lots of tears. Must be another side effect of pregnancy because she rarely cried, yet couldn't seem to stop today.

"Of course," she blabbered on. "That's making wild assumptions, isn't it? You might not even want me anymore now. I mean, after seeing me this morning and now." She hiccuped, wiped at her eyes with her free hand, thinking she probably looked pathetic with her red, wet eyes and runny nose from crying. "I really should just shut up, shouldn't I?"

Ty stared at her, shaking his head as he pulled her onto his lap and wrapped his arms around her. "Ellie, and I do mean Ellie because you do steal my breath, there is no one I want more than you. Haven't you figured that out yet?"

She sniffed. "Why would you want me, Ty?"

"Are you kidding me? Why wouldn't I?"

Should she write him a thesis? Or perhaps just send him the abbreviated version?

"You are a beautiful, intelligent, sexy, fun, wonderful, caring woman, and I know it, so you should, too."

Yep, she was dreaming, so she might as well enjoy her dream. She buried her face in his chest and let him hold her, let him soothe the part of her that had never quite felt good enough for her family.

In Ty's arms, she felt good enough.

She felt perfect.

She didn't know how the future would play out. For the moment the future didn't matter. All that mattered was that Ty made her feel complete, as if she belonged. He made her believe in herself, made her stronger than she'd thought she was.

CHAPTER ELEVEN

TY DREADED GOING downstairs, but knew eventually he would have to face his family. Part of him was surprised he and Ellie hadn't been interrupted by the whole Donaldson clan. Each of them would have something to say to him, no doubt.

Things he'd really rather Ellie not hear.

He'd convinced her to lie down. He'd lain down with her, held her sleeping body spooned up against him for almost an hour before he'd slipped out of the bed. He liked how her body fit against his, how holding her in his arms felt so right.

His brain had been racing from the moment he'd realized she might be pregnant. There were so many things to consider that he didn't want to rush what he said to her, didn't want to possibly say the wrong thing and inadvertently create problems.

A baby.

He'd dedicated his life to caring for babies, for nurturing and providing care for innocent new lives. Now he was going to be responsible for a new life.

A baby.

His and Ellie's baby.

Really, before he faced his family's various reactions, he'd like a little time to figure out his own emotions and to clear his head. Black Magic called to him. Big-time.

Somehow he made it out of the house without bumping into anyone, but the moment he stepped into the barn, his brother slapped him on the shoulder.

"Wanna go for a ride?" Harry asked, probably knowing that was exactly where Ty was headed.

"Absolutely." He went into a tack room, grabbed his saddle. When he'd gotten his gear, he wasn't surprised to see his brother had already mounted his stallion. Black Magic waited impatiently.

He spent a great deal of time getting the horse ready for the ride, taking time to talk gently to the stallion, to allow him to bond again with his too-long-gone master.

When he sat on the horse, old memories and emotions hit him. He'd loved this horse, but first medical school then moving to New York had kept him away.

But really what had kept him away had been much more than physical location and distance.

His father's disapproval had been what had driven him away.

In silence, he and his brother rode out across the fields, riding toward nowhere in particular, yet neither was surprised when they stopped at a pond where they'd often ridden out to, fished and played at as kids.

Although the air was brisk, the sun was shining and light glimmered across the water's surface.

"You wanna talk about it?" Harry asked when

they'd both dismounted and stood next to the pond just as they'd done hundreds of times in the past. They'd swum in this pond, played in this pond, camped at this pond.

Removing his gloves, Ty picked up a rock, skipped it over the water. One. Two. Three. Sink. He found another flat stone, tossed it toward the water. "Ellie's pregnant."

"Yeah, I heard." Harry bent and studied the ground until he found a rock that suited him. "My wife isn't known for her discretion, God love her."

Ty shrugged. "Mom already knew."

"Mom has this way of already knowing everything." Harry gave his stone a fling and it skipped farther out than Ty's had gone. "So, what are you going to do? You going to marry her?"

"I'm not sure." He wasn't even sure that if he wanted to get married whether Ellie would marry him. She didn't need some man complicating her life. Not that he hadn't already complicated her life enough by getting her pregnant.

"Her father will likely get out his shotgun when he finds out."

"His proverbial one, maybe," Harry agreed. "I may not know Senator Aston, but I do know of him. Shooting you would cost him too many votes, so I think you're safe."

Despite his brother's teasing tone, Ty didn't smile. "She deserves better than me. A lot better."

Harry stopped in midsearch for another stone, looked up at him and frowned. "Because she's an Aston?"

"Because she's Ellie." Which summed up everything. He couldn't care less that she was an Aston. What he cared about was the woman herself. He cared about Ellie.

Straightening, Harry seemed to consider his answer. "She could do worse."

"Yeah." Ty gave the stone he'd been holding a hard fling. "She could have ended up with you."

Harry grinned. "Nah, Nita wouldn't have been happy 'bout that. I'm a taken man." His brother hit his shoulder. "It's not so bad, you know. Having a kid, being married. You might like it."

"This coming from the man who still lives with his parents." Ty could have bitten his tongue off the moment the words had left his mouth.

Harry's face paled, then his cheeks splotched red, and not from the cold.

"I didn't mean that the way it sounded."

"Sure you did," his brother countered, cramming his hands into his jacket pockets. "In some ways, you're right. I do live in that big house with Mom and Dad, because you know what? I love it there. I love having my wife and child grow up on this ranch, because I love it here. I love Swallow Creek, the Triple D, and there's no place on earth I'd rather be than right here with my family."

Ty didn't say anything. He figured he'd already said too much.

"But that life isn't for you," his brother surprised him by saying. "The ranch has never been in your blood the way it has in Dad's and mine. William's, too, actually. But living on this ranch isn't what I was referring to. I was talking about having a family, a place where you belong."

That Ty understood. "I belong at the Angel Mendez Children's Hospital."

"Really?" Harry's brows formed a V and he sank down on a fallen log, picked at a piece of loose moss before glancing up and meeting Ty's gaze. "That's enough? Your career?"

"It always has been."

"Before Ellie."

Before Ellie. The words seemed to echo across the plains, strumming louder and louder in Ty's head.

"She's a part of Angel's," he said slowly, wondering why the words wouldn't quit sounding through his mind. *Before Ellie.*

"Ellie is your family, Ty. She's carrying your baby."

Ty sank onto the log next to his brother. "Tell me about it."

"So, I ask you again," Harry said with that calm big-brother voice of reason of his. "What are you going to do? You need a game plan, bro.

Because we both know that when Dad finds out you've gotten a Northern girl pregnant out of wedlock, he's going to hit the roof."

"Of all the stupid, irresponsible stunts that boy has pulled, this one tops them all!"

Ty winced. Yep, Harry had been right. His father was hitting the roof. Ty had barely stepped back into the house from his ride with his brother and didn't really have his game plan formed. He'd wanted to talk to Ellie prior to doing that. To tell her his thoughts and how he felt about her, to ask what her thoughts were, what she was feeling.

Unfortunately, he doubted he was going to get the opportunity. At least, not before a confrontation with his father.

His mother replied in her usual steady voice, encouraging her husband to calm down, that having another grandchild was a good thing.

Good ole mom, always coming to his defense.

"The boy is living in New York City. What kind of place is that to even consider raising a family? Too many people, too much pollution, no grass to grow beneath one's feet."

Ty felt his father's shudder as much as he heard it.

"And rather than have a real man's job, he takes care of babies for a living." Another shudder, this one much more pronounced. "What kind of example is that going to be for my grandchild?"

A new jab poked into an old wound. Hadn't this been exactly the argument that had led him into leaving Swallow Creek? Into swearing he wouldn't return? He didn't have to be a rancher to be a real man.

Except in his father's eyes, that was.

Ty took a deep breath and prepared to go into the kitchen where his parents were talking. Might as well get this over with rather than leave his mother to take all the flak.

No doubt she'd taken enough of that over the years since he had moved away.

"A good one."

Pausing in midstep on his way into the room,

Ty's ears perked up at the steady voice that responded to his father's question.

Not his mother's voice, as he'd expected, but Ellie's.

"What did you say?" His father's voice boomed, obviously shocked and awed that someone dared speak up.

Ellie's voice didn't waver, neither did it stutter. God bless her. "I said Ty would be a good example for our child."

His father harrumphed. "A good example would be for that boy to get his act together and get his butt home so he can help take care of family responsibilities."

Without so much as a pause, he heard Ellie's sweet voice continue to defend him.

"He has new family responsibilities now. To me and our baby."

"To you? Hell, woman, he's not even got a ring on your finger and you're knocked up. I don't think he can be accused of facing his family responsibilities or doing right by you."

Ty cringed, wondered why he was still standing just outside the room, yet he wanted to hear what Ellie would say. He needed to hear what she would say.

"Ty is a man of honor."

His heart swelled at her confident words. God, he would do his best to do right by her. Somehow. Some way. He would do right by Ellie and their baby.

"A man of honor doesn't abandon his family to move out of state to take care of babies."

"A man I admire and respect," she continued as if his father hadn't spoken. "A man who works hard and gives all he has to help those around him, a man who will be a good father and not judge our child based upon outdated, chauvinistic ideas that a man has to live off the land to be a real man."

Pride surged at Ellie's staunch defense. Knowing how her anxiety tended to flare, he was again amazed that not once had she stuttered. Hell, he'd seen his father make grown men stutter and quake in their boots. Yet Ellie was standing her ground, defending *him*.

Ty closed his eyes, picturing her in his mind, her smile, her eyes, the way she looked at him when he kissed her.

The way he knew he looked at her. As if she meant the world to him.

Because she did.

"You've known him, what, a few months? Don't pretend you know my son better than I do."

"Harold, don't do this," Ty's mother begged, speaking up for the first time since Ellie had come into the conversation. "Don't say such things."

"You know I'm right. That foolhardy boy always had his nose in a book when he should have been doing other things."

"Other things such as being like you, Dad?" Ty hadn't consciously decided to step out of the shadows, but he couldn't risk his father launching into Ellie. He wouldn't risk it. She was too fragile.

Too precious.

As timid as she'd always been around the hospital, recalling how panicked she'd been at the ribbon-cutting ceremony, he was amazed at how she'd defended him, at how her shoulders were high and her gaze bright, confident. Had she been wearing a long red cape and the wind blowing in her hair, he wouldn't have been surprised. Ellie was his heroine.

His father's lips pursed and his gaze narrowed as it settled on Ty. "A boy could do worse than to grow up to be like his old man."

True. His father was a hardworking man who had always provided for his family, had always given as much as he demanded of others. But that didn't mean Ty had to follow in his footsteps.

"I'm not like you, Dad."

"Ty," his mother began, her nervous gaze going back and forth between her husband and her younger son, "perhaps we should have this conversation later."

"Why, so that we can sugarcoat the fact that my own father is disappointed in me?" Had he ever said those words out loud before? He didn't think so. Maybe he'd never even mentally acknowledged them, but something about Ellie's defense of him made him acknowledge a lot of things.

"No, thanks. We've been doing that for years and it's not helped one bit. And if it's for Ellie's benefit, don't bother. She's already seen how he feels about me. Hearing the words only confirms what she has already figured out."

"Don't you be rude to your mother, boy."

"I'm not a boy," he countered, not really thinking he'd been rude to his mother and certainly not intending to have disrespected her in any way. But his father's chest puffed up and his gaze narrowed.

Out of years of deferring to the man he'd been taught his whole life to respect, Ty automatically zipped his lips.

Ellie, on the other hand, did not.

"He's right," she said with that easy confidence again that surprised him. "Ty is a man. A very good man who is going to be a father. A very good father to our baby, who can grow up and do anything he or she likes in life, whether that be a baby doctor or a rancher or a garbage collector. What's important is that our child grow up healthy and happy and knowing that he or she can do or accomplish anything and that self-worth does not come from how others see you but how one sees oneself."

Ty bit back a smile at the shocked look crossing his father's face and took a step forward in Ellie's direction. Hell, he wanted to wrap his arms around her and spin her around for the staunch way she defended him.

But she was oblivious to him and focused solely on his father. Her shoulders lifted, her eyes burned with dark intensity and she met his father's gaze squarely.

"If you want anything to do with our baby, you will learn to appreciate the wonderful man you have for a son because he is a brilliant doctor and an honorable man," she warned, her hands on her hips and her expression serious. "I will not have my child around someone who obviously has so little appreciation for a man who does so much good for so many."

Blood pounding in her ears, Eleanor wondered if Ty was going to read her the riot act for daring to be so outspoken to his father, but she didn't care at the moment. Anger burned too hotly in her veins for her to hold her tongue. Really, how could any man be so obtuse?

No wonder Ty had moved so far away.

She'd awakened, realized Ty was gone, and that he must have been for some time because the bed barely held an imprint of him having been there. She'd gone downstairs to find him.

And stumbled on Ty's parents, discussing him.

Discussing being the mildest of ways she knew how to put what Ty's father had been doing.

Degrading his son.

Tearing him down.

She hadn't been able to stand it.

How dared he say such things about the most wonderful man she had ever known? About the man who made her view life differently?

If the blustery old man thought he was going to have anything to do with her baby when he treated his son so callously, he was wrong.

Because she might have only known she was pregnant for a few hours, but she loved this baby and would protect him or her with her life. No way would she let some overbearing, pompous man berate her child.

Or her child's father.

"Ellie, dear, perhaps you and I should go to the den and let the men have this discussion?" Ty's mother suggested gently, her worried gaze going back and forth between her son and her husband. She moved toward Ellie, put her arm gently on her shoulder.

Eleanor risked a look at Ty. His face was dark, cloudy, upset.

Coldness doused the flame that burned within her.

She had overstepped her boundaries.

Hadn't she known she had?

She might be pregnant with Ty's baby, but she'd

been talking to his father. Blood was thicker than water. Didn't that always hold true?

Still, she wasn't going to apologize. Not when she so strongly disagreed with how Ty's father treated him.

"Actually, I need to do some things upstairs," she ventured, not wanting to go with Ty's mother so that she could be scolded for overstepping her place. Plus, tears burned at her eyes and she wanted to get away, far away, before they fell. No way did she want to show weakness in front of this family. If for no other reason, she didn't want them to think they could browbeat her in regard to her baby. They couldn't. She held her head high. "If you'll excuse me…"

Without pausing, she headed back toward the stairs she'd descended only minutes before.

She hadn't mentally made any decisions, but when she got back to Ty's room, saw all the things from his childhood and past, she was struck with homesickness.

Immense and utter homesickness.

Perhaps her family was odd. Perhaps they each

had their own quirks and faults. But they were her family.

She wanted them.

Before she even consciously thought about what she was doing, she had her suitcase out of Ty's closet and had begun methodically packing her things back into the case.

"What are you doing?"

She spun at the sound of Ty's voice. "Going home."

Filling the entire doorway with his tall frame and broad shoulders, he didn't look happy. His gaze narrowing, he stepped into the room, closed his bedroom door behind him.

"Why?" he asked, turning the lock.

She almost winced at the sound of the lock clicking into place. Why? Ha, did he really have to ask why she'd want to leave?

"Because I don't want to be here any longer." Truer words had never been spoken. She wanted to be far away from the Triple D ranch and Texas.

His hands on his hips, Ty stood just inside

the door, staring at her with an expression she couldn't quite read. "Because of what just happened downstairs?"

"Because I want to go home, Ty. I want to be back in the city, back at Angel's." Back where she belonged. "I don't like it here."

"This is my home."

"Yes, and hasn't it been a lovely homecoming for you?" She hadn't meant to be sarcastic or to say anything derogatory. Lord knew, he got enough of that from his father. But the words had slipped out before she could stop them.

His lips tightened. "With the exception of my father, yes, it has been."

Exactly. The rest of his family had been quite lovely. She shouldn't have said what she had. Shame filled her. Shame and frustration and the overwhelming need to be in her own environment, to have time to process all the things that had happened over the past few days, over the past few weeks since Ty had rescued her at the ribbon-cutting.

Her entire life had turned topsy-turvy.

Her life would never be the same again.

She was going to be a mother, to have Ty's baby.

"Well, good for you." She forced a tight smile to her lips, pretended she wasn't falling apart on the inside, because really she wanted to be strong. "I'm glad that you have had a good visit, but I want to go home."

He stared at her as if he was looking at a stranger. "We're not supposed to leave for another two days, Ellie."

"Don't call me that!"

The name did her in. Emotions were battling within her and hearing him call her that when the single word could bring her so far down or so high up thanks to him was just too much.

"But—"

"No buts, I've asked and asked you not to call me that, but you're just like your father. You think you know what's best for other people so you do what you want anyway. Even when that person has asked you repeatedly not to call her that." Over twenty years' worth of frustrations and hurt spewed forth all at once. "Well, guess what? I don't like it, so don't!"

"What's wrong with you, Eleanor?"

The way he enunciated her name grated on her nerves like fingernails on a chalkboard. "Nothing."

"Is this about the pregnancy? It's normal for you to feel emotional."

Emotional? Yes, she felt emotional. Overflowing with emotions. All of which centered around the man staring at her as if he wasn't quite sure what to think.

"Sure, I'm probably just hormonal." She actually felt hormonal. She felt overwhelmed. Sad. As if every nerve ending in her body was in motion.

He raked his fingers through his hair, leaving dark tufts in disarray. "I don't understand what's going on, why you're doing this."

She glanced at the open suitcase on the bed. "I'm packing my bags so I can go home. I don't want to be here. I don't want to be with you. I just want to go home. Now."

He flinched almost as if she'd struck him. His lips tightened to a thin line. He sighed, seemed to come to some decision. "Fine, I'll have Harry fly you to the airport. If he can't because of the rodeo, I'll fly us there." At her look of alarm, he added, "It's been a while, but I have my pilot's license. Harry and I took lessons at the same time during our teens and have flown since." He paused, stared straight into her eyes. "You're sure this is what you want?"

At the moment, leaving was the only thing she was sure of. She needed to be moving, to be taking action, to soothe the anxiety rising within her that was threatening to go into a full-blown panic attack, to get home to where she could dissect the emotions rushing through her.

"Get me home, Ty." She wanted to be as far away from Texas as she could possibly get. New York sounded just about perfect.

She watched walls slide into place as he shielded his emotions behind an expression she'd never seen on his face before. One almost of indifference.

"Fine." He sounded as if he couldn't care less, that what she did didn't matter to him and he'd just as soon she leave as stay. "You want to go home. I'll get you home."

CHAPTER TWELVE

ELEANOR SAT ON Ty's bed, uncertain about what she needed to do. He'd disappeared more than thirty minutes ago, saying he'd be back for her when the plane was ready. She'd finished packing and had been sitting on the bed ever since.

A light knock sounded on Ty's door. Much lighter than Ty would have done. Not that he'd have knocked to enter his own bedroom anyway.

Although she didn't want to face anyone, she refused to show any remorse over her confrontation with Ty's father. She'd meant every word.

"Ellie," Ty's mother called through the door. "May I please come in? Please."

Taking a deep breath, Eleanor crossed the room, opened the door and moved aside for the woman to enter.

When inside the room she looked as uncomfortable as Eleanor felt.

"I suppose you think my husband is terrible."

Eleanor didn't speak. Really, what could she say?

"He isn't. He was just raised a certain way and sees the world in black-and-white with no shades of gray."

"Ty being a doctor isn't a shade of gray."

His mother smiled, surprising Eleanor. "I heard the two of you argue. I wasn't intentionally eavesdropping. I came to find you, to tell you how happy I am Ty has a strong woman like you."

Eleanor wanted to laugh. Her, strong? Ha. Ty's mother had her confused with someone else.

"So the fact that even now you defend him, well, it makes this mother's heart sing with joy." Then she surprised Eleanor even further by wrapping her arms around her. "Please reconsider leaving. My son loves you. Stay and talk this out with him."

Eleanor reeled at the woman's words. "Ty doesn't love me."

She supposed the woman might think that as

he'd brought her here when he'd never brought a woman home. Then there was the whole thing of being pregnant with his baby.

"Has he not told you?" Then his mother frowned. "Have you told him how you feel? That you're in love with him?"

"I don't love Ty," she denied, but even as she said the words, she realized that she did.

That perhaps on the night he'd rescued her at the ribbon-cutting she'd fallen hopelessly in love with Ty Donaldson.

Standing just inside the open door of his bedroom, Ty recalled exactly why he'd been taught not to eavesdrop.

He flinched at the words that stopped him cold.

Hearing Ellie say she didn't love him cut straight through his chest, right to the soft center of his heart.

Hell, he was making a habit of eavesdropping today and nothing good had come out of it yet.

Squaring his shoulders, he cleared his throat.

Both women spun toward him.

"Ty!" Ellie gasped, her face flushing, her eyes bright, guilty. Guilty because she didn't love him and he'd heard her say so.

Thank God he hadn't poured his sappy heart out to her earlier.

"The plane is fueled up and Harry is going to fly you to Houston. I've booked you a seat on the first available flight back to New York."

Her gaze dropped, then she nodded. "Thank you."

"Ty," his mother said, stepping toward him, "I was just trying to convince Ellie to stay. Don't you think that's a good idea?"

"Her name is Eleanor and, no, I don't think her staying is a good idea at all." Never would he be accused of forcing a woman to be with him when she'd so plainly said she didn't want to be.

His mother let out a loud sigh. "You're as stubborn as your father." With a shake of her head she hugged Ellie. "For whatever it's worth, I hope you change your mind and decide to stay. This family needs to heal and you started that process today. Please don't leave without seeing it through."

Heal? His mother thought what had happened between him and his father had been healing? Wrong. The confrontation had been like ripping the scab off a deep wound. Nothing more.

Looking torn, Eleanor hugged his mother back. "Thank you for welcoming me into your home." She hesitated. "With the baby, I'm sure our paths will cross in the future. Please take care." Then she turned to Ty. "I'm ready to go."

She reached for her suitcase, but Ty beat her to it.

"No way am I letting you carry that."

"I'm pregnant, not an invalid."

He shrugged. "Makes no difference. You're not carrying it."

When they reached the bottom of the stairs, Ty's mother stopped them.

"You can't leave without saying goodbye to William. He'd be heartbroken."

Yeah, well, his nephew wasn't the only one who was going to be heartbroken when Ellie left.

"He's in the pool. I'll go get him if you'll wait?"

Eleanor nodded.

She and Ty stood in silence, then she sighed.

"We should have just walked out to the pool instead of her having to drag William inside."

She nodded, sure he was right.

"Ty!" His mother's scream echoed through the house.

Both Ty and Eleanor took off toward the door that led out to the pool.

What met their gazes made Eleanor's stomach tighten into a nervous ball.

Ty's father was in the pool, holding a lifeless little body to his chest but apparently frozen with fear and unable to move further.

Ty immediately jumped to action, crossing the distance and jumping into the pool.

"Give him to me," he demanded of his father.

His pain-filled eyes dropping to the lax body of his grandson, he did so.

Ty took William, prayed he wasn't too late, assessed him while carrying him from the pool.

As best as he could tell, there wasn't any

trauma or neck injuries. God, he hoped William hadn't dived into the pool, injured his neck, been paralyzed and drowned.

But his nephew had drowned.

No heartbeat. No respirations.

A pain unlike any Ty had ever experienced slashed across his chest, but he drew on years of experience with dealing with medical emergencies to move automatically.

"Oh, Ty," Ellie cried, as he laid William's tiny body on the concrete and began performing cardiopulmonary resuscitation.

Ellie pulled her cell phone from her purse, dialed 911 and realized she had no idea what Ty's address was.

"The Triple D Ranch," she told the emergency worker. "We're at the Triple D Ranch."

Behind her, Ty's mother gave the address and Ellie carefully repeated it to the voice on the other end of the phone line.

She handed the phone to Ty's mother and bent

beside him, meaning to help him with the CPR, but her gaze caught on Ty's father.

The man still stood in the pool. She didn't think he'd budged since he'd handed William over to Ty.

Worried that more might be going on than just shock, she called out his name, but he didn't even look her way.

Kicking off her shoes, Ellie went into the pool to Harold Donaldson.

"Mr. Donaldson?" She touched his arm.

He jumped, seeming to come out of the trance he'd been in. He glanced around, his eyes landing on where Ty was working on William.

"I didn't know what to do," he began, his voice trembling.

Despite her differences with the man, her heart squeezed with compassion. She put her arm around him. "Come on. Let's get you out of the pool."

Ty counted compressions in his head, gave a breath at the appropriate times and prayed. In his mind, he prayed and prayed and prayed.

But nothing happened.

No lub-dub of William's heart.

No gasp of breath or sputtering or cough.

Nothing.

He couldn't let this happen. Couldn't not revive William.

Couldn't ever forget the pallid color on his father's face, the pain in his father's eyes as he'd taken William out of his shaking arms.

Never had Ty seen a weak link in his father's armor. Never had he seen the man not know exactly what to do.

His father was a man of action, a decisive man who never questioned, just did.

Ty gave another breath.

Nothing.

The longer he couldn't revive William the less likely he was to be able to.

How long had the boy been in the pool? How long had his father just been holding his lifeless body?

From the corner of his eye he saw his mother go to his father, wrap her arms around him and start talking to him. He saw Ellie reassure herself that nothing more was wrong with his father than fear, then she moved to him, knelt next to where he desperately tried to save William.

"Let me help." She didn't wait for him to answer, just bent and gave William a breath, counted his compressions out loud and repeated the breath.

And a miracle happened.

Nothing could convince Ty that anything short of a miracle had happened.

Because William coughed.

Weakly at first, then stronger as his lungs cleared the water.

"Oh, Ty, he's alive."

At Ellie's exclamation, Ty's mother cried out and his father sank to his knees.

"Harold!" His wife sank down next to him.

"Check him," he ordered Ellie, not willing to leave William's side but afraid the stress of what had happened might be affecting his father's heart.

William's eyes opened, he coughed more. Deep, rattling coughs that shook his tiny frame.

Ty turned him, beat on his back, trying to assist in clearing the fluid.

"Uncle Ty?"

Ty let out the breath he hadn't realized he'd been holding.

Stepping out of the house, Harry and Nita took in the scene before them.

"What the hell is going on here?"

Eleanor could recall very few times of sitting in a hospital waiting area. At least, from her current point of view as an anxious family member waiting to hear news.

Family member.

She wasn't really family.

But the baby inside her was William's cousin, was a part of this family.

She glanced at Ty. He sat slumped over, eyes closed. He'd barely said a word to her since they'd followed the ambulance to the hospital. His mother had sat in the front seat next to him and she and Nita had shared the backseat of the king cab Triple D pickup. Harry had ridden in the ambulance with his son and father.

When they'd arrived, Ty's mother had been allowed to stay with her husband while he was checked over just to make sure his reaction had only been one of stress. Harry and Nita were both with William. Which left Eleanor and Ty alone in the emergency room waiting area.

Ty opened his eyes, caught her watching him. His expression tightened. "I'm sorry you missed your flight."

"Really? You think I'm worried about my flight?"

"I thought you were all set to get out of Texas as quickly as possible."

Eleanor's eyes closed and she prayed for strength to see her through the rest of this stressful day. "I thought you were upset with me and I panicked."

"Why the hell would I have been upset with you?"

"Because of what I said to your father."

"When you defended me? Hell, darlin', I thought you were great. Brilliant. I didn't want you to leave."

"You weren't upset?"

"At you? Never," he answered without hesitation. "My father is a different story altogether. Hell, we'll both just leave. I'll go back to New York with you."

"But the rodeo—"

"The rodeo was just an excuse to get me home," he interrupted, sitting up in his seat. "My mother hoped my father and I would work things out, but that's never going to happen. We're too different. He is never going to understand me and I quit trying to make him understand years ago."

He stood, moved next to where she sat.

"Thank you for trying, though, Ellie."

Ellie. He'd called her Ellie.

That's all it took for the dam of emotions to break loose within Eleanor. She'd been holding them at bay so staunchly, trying to be strong during all the afternoon's drama, but hearing the nickname destroyed all her resolve.

Because when Ty had called her Eleanor earlier, she'd hurt. Deep down hurt.

Because she wasn't Eleanor.

Not with Ty.

She was Ellie.

Not Jelly Ellie, but Ellie, the woman who stole Ty Donaldson's breath.

Because when he looked at her, said her name, that's exactly how he made her feel. As if she really did steal his breath.

Just as he was looking at her right this moment.

"I didn't mean to make you cry." He touched her face, brushed away tears that she hadn't realized had fallen. "I'm sorry, Ellie. Sorry you had to deal with my father. Sorry you want to leave. Sorry you don't love me."

The last one had her looking up at him. "Why would that matter?"

He gave a soft laugh. "What my mother said earlier was right."

He knew she loved him? "But how?"

He brushed his thumb across her cheek. "How could I not?"

She supposed he saw the truth in her eyes every time she looked at him, every time she'd kissed him, touched him.

Because she did love him. Even now the way she felt about him was probably shining in her eyes.

"I'm sorry, Ty. I didn't mean it to happen."

"It's not your fault."

Perhaps not, but she didn't want him feeling sorry for her. Which apparently was what was happening. He'd overheard what his mother had said and was taking pity on her just as he'd done at the ribbon-cutting.

Or maybe he was just being nice because of the baby.

Either way, she didn't want his pity. She wanted his heart.

"I know you didn't intend me to fall in love with you. I just did."

As Ty's words registered, the room spun

around Ellie and she worried for a brief moment that she might pass out again. "You fell in love with me?"

He gave an ironic laugh. "As I said, how could I not? You're wonderful, Ellie."

"But I thought…" Her voice trailed off, a thousand thoughts hitting her at once. That Ty loved her was the foremost one. Ty was in love with her. "You really love me?"

"It's okay, Ellie." He shrugged off her question. "I heard what you told my mother. It's not a big deal."

He started to turn away but she grabbed his arm. "Ty Donaldson, it's a very big deal. If you love me, it's the biggest deal of my entire life."

Facing her, he searched her eyes, his soft and vulnerable as understanding dawned. A lopsided grin lifted one corner of his mouth. "Oh, really? The biggest deal, eh?"

"Really," she said, hope building higher and higher within her at how he was looking at her, at what she saw shining brightly in his eyes.

He stood, pulled her to her feet. "I love you, Eleanor Aston."

Her heart burst with joy at his words, but she shook her head. "Not acceptable."

His smile fell.

"Tell me again," she demanded, staring up at him. "Only this time get it right."

It only took Ty a second to realize exactly what she meant. Taking her hands in his, he stared straight into her eyes, straight into her heart. "I love you, Ellie Aston."

She smiled. "Much better."

"Agreed." He grinned, pulling her into his arms. "I've never understood why you protested so much anyway. Ellie fits you."

Knowing the past no longer mattered, she told him about "Jelly Ellie," watching as anger darkened his expression.

"Whoever called you that has a lot to answer for and had better hope like hell they never have the misfortune of crossing my path."

She smiled. "The name doesn't bother me anymore, Ty. When you called me Eleanor earlier, it…" Her voice broke and she shrugged helplessly. "It tore me to bits because I'm not Eleanor anymore. I'm Ellie and I like who that woman is because she's your woman."

"Always, Ellie. You're always going to be mine." With those words, he kissed her. The sweetest, most possessive kiss Eleanor had ever had the pleasure of experiencing.

"Tell me," he breathed against her lips. "Say the words to me."

Placing her palms on each side of his face and staring directly into his beautiful eyes, she smiled. "I love you, Ty Donaldson. Always and forever."

"I like the sound of that."

"Ahem."

Both Ty and Ellie spun at the sound of his father clearing his throat.

"Dad."

Ellie didn't have to be a rocket scientist to hear the relief in Ty's voice.

No wonder. His father's normal robust color

was back and he looked fit enough to take on the world. Thank God.

"They tell me they are going to keep William overnight for observation but that he's going to be just fine."

Ty nodded. That's what Harry had told them earlier, too.

An awkward silence filled the lobby as the three of them stood there, no one saying anything.

"Perhaps I should step out. Get a cup of coffee." Remembering her pregnancy, she changed it to, "A glass of juice or something."

As she went to step past Ty's father, he grabbed her arm. "No, young lady, you need to hear this. Have a seat."

Young lady? Ellie winced. Was Ty's father really going to start in while they were in the emergency room waiting area?

Ty glared at his father's hands on Ellie's arm. He wasn't one bit surprised when she failed to sit, though. Ellie was developing quite a backbone.

But she didn't need it.

Because if his father thought for one minute that Ty was going to let him say one negative thing to Ellie, one negative thing to him, he was wrong.

Not today. Not ever again.

"Calm down, son," Harold ordered, apparently reading Ty's expression correctly. "And have a seat because I have something I need to say and you need to hear this. Both of you need to hear it."

A war waged within Ty, but he sat, taking Ellie's hand as she sat in the seat next to him. He couldn't say he liked his father towering over them, but he'd had a long day so Ty would give him that advantage.

"I know we've had our differences."

To put it mildly.

"But what you did today…" His father paused, looked every one of his years as he met Ty's gaze. "Son, I was wrong."

Ty's breath caught. Ellie's hand squeezed his. Was his father saying what he thought he was?

"My whole life I've thought I knew what was

best for you boys, what was right, but today you proved to me what a fool I've been."

"I just did my job."

"Exactly. A job that I've never given you any credit for. Just as I never told you I was proud of how well you did with your studies and medical school."

From the corner of his eye he saw Ellie dab at her eyes. Ty clenched his teeth, determined he would not let his father's words get to him.

"But I was always proud of you, Ty. Proud that no matter what anyone said you went after your dreams and the rest of the world could take it or leave it. I was proud that you were your own man with your own mind and that you aced everything you did."

Ty wanted to hit the side of his head to clear his ears, because he was certain he hadn't heard correctly.

"Today, what you did, Ty, son, I can't begin to tell you how in awe I am of what you do, of how proud I am of the fine doctor you are."

A tiny sob escaped Ellie. Her fingers dug into his.

"I…" He glanced around the empty lobby. "Well, that's all I came to say. That I am proud of you and I'm sorry for not telling you sooner."

He turned to leave the lobby but Ty stopped him, wrapping his arms around his father's stiff body.

But after just a second Harold took over the hug in true Harold Donaldson fashion and hugged Ty so tightly that he could barely breathe.

When his father had left the lobby, Ty turned Ellie and pulled her to him.

"Did you say something about being mine for always and forever, darlin'?" he asked, holding her close to him.

"Seems like I recall saying something along those lines." Ellie smiled, knowing that always and forever with Ty sounded about as close to heaven on earth as one could get.

EPILOGUE

"You ready for this?"

Checking to make sure his tuxedo was straight, Ty grinned at his brother. "I've been ready for this for months."

"Yeah, a shame it took you that long to convince the bride to make an honest man of you."

It had taken him way too long to convince Ellie to marry him. "Stubborn woman wouldn't agree until after Levi was born."

"Yes, because every woman wants to be pregnant in her wedding photos."

Ty could have pointed out that he'd have marched Ellie down the aisle on the day he'd first told her he loved her, on the day that she'd first told him she loved him.

He'd known he wanted to spend the rest of his life with her. In the months that passed, he'd not changed his mind or his heart. The way he felt about Ellie just kept growing, getting stronger with each day that passed.

Ty and Harry joined the rest of the wedding party on the lawn of the Triple D. Row after row of white chairs were filled with Texans in their best Sunday duds and New Yorkers in the latest European fashions.

His father held Levi in the front row. Ty grinned at the tiny white Stetson that his dad had insisted the six- month-old wear. William fidgeted next to Harry, toying with the ring pillow he held.

The live band began to play the wedding march and all eyes, especially Ty's, went to where Ellie rode up in a white carriage with crushed red velvet seats. Her beaming newly reelected to the Senate father stepped up to the carriage and assisted his lovely daughter down.

Ty's breath caught at the beautiful woman who would officially become his during this ceremony. In reality, she'd been his from the moment they declared their love and he'd been hers.

He took in her long dark hair in a mass of curls

about her neck and cascading down her back. Her gown was strapless and accented her beautiful curves and nipped- in waist. Never had a bride been more beautiful.

Never had a woman been more loved.

Her gaze met Ty's and she smiled.

A smile that told him everything words never could convey.

A smile that told of a love that would last always and forever.

* * * * *